Confessions of a Lapsed St

'I am hard pressed to think
captures the essence of the
such telling economy . . . Th wn
Russian life are beautifully ca akine is a
master word-painter and, even in translation, you can
admire his precise brush work. It is less than 150 pages
long, but it has the panoramic sweep of the great
Russian novels of the nineteenth century'
David Robson, *Sunday Telegraph*

'It is easy to understand Makine's success. He writes
lyrically, with an intensity that appeals to all our senses.
He is adept at evoking both the everyday – men playing
dominoes in the courtyard – and the extraordinary'
Robert Chandler, *Independent*

'Its main concern is with those moments when the
communist dream becomes lost in the mists of time and
disappointment . . . However, Makine is not interested in
a sweeping panorama of the failures of the Soviet project.
His gaze is focused squarely on the ordinary man in
the street to whom the post-war dream meant
everything – a visionary gleam that would excuse the
hunger and hardship and which most democratic citizens
would think blinkered . . . The power Makine's prose
creates comes from the vivid sense of nostalgia he
builds when evoking his home town set against its
slow disintegration'
Gary Atkinson, *Glasgow Herald*

'A perfect gem on a par with Schlink's THE READER or Mulrooney's ARABY, a short, beautifully formed, poetic tale of growing up in the hardship of '60s Russia, where life is an adventure and the past is for grown-ups only. That is, until the narrator too becomes grown up, listens to his parents' history and experiences Afghanistan. A truly memorable work that deeply affected me'
Sarah Broadhurst, *Bookseller*

'There is a poetic economy to the prose style in this brief story of two boys growing up in post World War II Russia. The style seems to illuminate even more brightly that which goes unsaid, as they play the drums and trumpet in a band that sets off every summer to march towards the bright dawn of the new Soviet Union. In the same way, although the rose tint of memory has made every detail of their lives in the collective housing compound seem fantastic and heroic, it only makes the slender minutiae of how their parents survived the wounds of the war even more tragic. Written in the early 90s – as a letter from one to the other when they have long grown up and emigrated to the west – this is a book that speaks as much about Russian emigrés today as it does of a time long gone'
Thom Dibdin, *List*

Confessions of a Lapsed Standard-Bearer

Andreï Makine

Translated by Geoffrey Strachan

SCEPTRE

Originally published in 1992 as *Confession d'un Porte-Drapeau Déchu*
by Editions Belfond, 12 Avenue d'Italie, 75013 Paris, France
This English translation first published in Great Britain in 2000 by
Hodder and Stoughton
A division of Hodder Headline
A Sceptre Paperback

10 9 8 7 6 5 4 3 2 1

A CIP cataloque record for this title is available from the British
Library.

ISBN 0 340 72809 4

Typeset by Hewer Text Ltd, Edinburgh
Printed and bound in Great Britain by Clays Ltd, St Ives plc, Bungay,
Suffolk

Hodder and Stoughton
A division of Hodder Headline
338 Euston Road
London NW1 3BH

TRANSLATOR'S NOTE

Andreï Makine was born and brought up in Russia but *Confessions of a Lapsed Standard-Bearer*, like his other novels, was written in French. Most of the book is set in Russia and the author uses some Russian words in the French text which I have kept in this English translation, these include: *izba* (a traditional wooden house built of logs); *babushka* (a grandmother); *soviet* (an elected local or national council in the former USSR), *shapka* (a fur hat or cap, often with ear flaps).

In conversation the characters sometimes allude to well-known historic names and to some specifically associated with the Communist period. The Nevsky Prospekt is the principal avenue in St Petersburg (Leningrad); the Sedov ice-breaker was named after the navigator and arctic explorer Georgyi Sedov; the Smolny is the building in Leningrad (once a girls' school) from which Lenin launched the October Revolution, and for many years the regional headquarters of the Communist party; Kliment Yefremovich Voroshilov was responsible, as commissar for defence (from 1925 to 1940), for the modernization of the Red Army and became President of the USSR from 1953 to 1960; Nikolay Ivanovich Yezhov was responsible, as head of the secret police (NKVD) from 1936 to 1938, for the most severe purges; Belomor is a brand of very strong Russian cigarette with no filters; Treptow Park in East Berlin contains monuments erected under the Communist regime after the Second World War including a statue of a Russian soldier rescuing a little German girl.

I am indebted to a number of people, including the author, for advice, assistance and encouragement in the preparation of this translation. To all of them my thanks are due, notably Malcolm Borthwick, Ludmilla Checkley, June Elks, Eric Haslam, Claire Squires, Simon Strachan, Susan Strachan and, above all, my editor at Sceptre, Carole Welch.

G.S.

for Marie-Claude
for Guy

It was all so simple. Crystal clear . . .

The bugle flung out its piercing calls. The drum reverberated. And so, too, high above its taut yellow skin, did the sky, whose wide tracts of fresh blue we drank in as we sang our lusty songs. Those drum rolls and those bugle calls shook the whole universe.

At the start of our lives it was all so clear. Our childhood had the tangy smell of gleaming brass, the martial resonance of a hardened drumskin.

And we marched along country roads with a bloom of dust on our legs. Always straight ahead. Always towards the radiant horizon.

Half the land was decked out with a dark lacework of barbed wire fences. Pinned to the ground by watchtowers. But as we marched along we believed it was advancing with us, this land of ours, towards the final goal, towards that horizon, already so close.

There was I, contorting my lungs so that

the old bugle should belch forth in a sparkling cascade the bellowing sound that to us was life itself, the *joie de vivre* of the half-starved children of the post-war era.

There were you, with your head tilted and your soft, dark eyes lost in the distance, raining down a brisk hail from your drumsticks onto the resonant skin.

Now we know all about it . . . Those country roads were simply corridors between broad zones fenced in with barbed wire. Watchtowers lurked behind the forests. They marched us round in circles to make us feel we were advancing. Now we know . . .

Amid all this ardent and incessant marching, like some blissful delirium, there was a port of anchorage: our courtyard. In the evening we would cross it. Without songs or drum rolls. Having done our duty. Taken one more decisive step towards the radiant horizon. We would collapse onto its trampled grass. For a well-earned rest.

On the long summer evenings the windows in the three buildings that formed the bizarre triangle of our courtyard would all be open. We would hear the soft mingling of sounds that emanated from these bee-hives. The hiss of cooking oil on a paraffin stove, the reassuring tones of a radio announcer, the lisping melody of a gramophone record, a baby wailing on the ground floor. This tranquil buzz was punctuated by the dry clicking of the dominoes players slamming down their pieces onto the wooden table in the centre of the courtyard, beneath the poplar trees.

An angular face would appear at one of the second-floor windows. My mother. She would peer into the courtyard for a moment, screwing up her eyes against the orange rays of the sunset. Then she would call: 'Yasha!'

A man would get up from a bench beyond the damp clumps of dahlias, mark the place in his book with a twig, and make his way towards the main entrance. Totally bald and unbelievably pale, his cranium looked transparent. There were just a few silvery hairs curled low down on the nape of his neck. Passing close by us he would call out with jocular but firm gentleness: 'All right, you pioneers, time to go and wash!'

This was Yakov Zinger. Yasha. Your father.

A few moments later he would reappear in the main entrance. Walking slightly bent. Like someone going out of his way not to show that his burden is heavy. With small, nimble, taut steps. With an assumed agility.

On his back he would be carrying a man. The man clung to his shoulders with calm confidence, as children do. His trouser legs were knotted in broad double bows. This was Pyotr Yevdokimov, my father.

Depending on what was asked of him, Yasha would sometimes put him down at the dominoes players' table, sometimes on the bench invaded by the wild exuberance of the dahlias, where your father would normally read.

We would emerge from our blissful torpor, pick up our rucksacks, the bugle and the drum, and climb up into the communal hive filled with its hum of domesticity. We had to wait for our neighbour to finish her laundry so we could wash, then we would eat in a corner of the kitchen before sinking into sleep. The pale, feathery light of a white northern night settled around us. Its milky flurries dulled the brassy clamour of the bugle and the rattle of the drum in our heads. Often, through the first flakes of this opaline sleepiness, I would hear Yasha's footsteps as he came into our room with his passenger. He would set my father down and as he left he would weave several whispered words into my dreams: 'Right then, see you tomorrow. Good night!'

The flat you lived in was on the same landing.

Why, today of all days, have I been remembering all that fanatical marching of ours? By pure chance, it seems.

I suppose you know how Russians get their news here in the West? Someone in San Francisco receives a card from Munich. Surprised at this renewed contact through the post, he telephones Sydney. 'You remember So-and-So? Yes, we used to live practically next door to them, well, he's in Germany. No, not permanently . . .' Three months later a long letter from Sydney arrives in Paris, and in a hasty postscript mentions that such and such a person is in Munich . . .

It was the same with you. '. . . Yes, Arkady has left,' a transatlantic voice whispered in the earpiece. 'He phoned a friend from Moscow and said he was going . . . Where to? I think it was either Cleveland or Portland . . . I can't remember now . . .'

That 'Cleveland or Portland' rang briefly in my ear again. I had stopped at the hot, noisy Carrefour de l'Odéon in Paris. The coming and going at this crossroads renders one invisible. One can remain quite still. Keep one's gaze focused in the misty distance, on that past of ours, stranger than death. No one will pay any attention. One can even murmur softly, as I do now: 'You know, we shall always be those pioneers with our red scarves. For us the sun will always have that faint tang of brass and the sky the resonance of drum rolls. You can't be cured of it. You can't get over that bright horizon only a few days' march away. What's the point of lying to ourselves? We shall never be like the others, like normal people. For example, like that man I see getting into a smart car. He glides up to the steering wheel with all the smoothness of a bank card being swallowed by a cash machine. The well-upholstered interior simply swallows him. First an arm, tossing his jacket onto the seat, then a leg, then his head, and – snap! – as smoothly as you please, he slips into it, as if into the soft embrace of a mistress. Smiling, relaxed. With one hand on the wheel, holding a slim, brown cigar, the other keying in a telephone number from memory . . .

'We shall imitate them. We shall ape their coolness. We shall allow well-upholstered seats to swallow us with the same easy smiles. But at heart we shall always remain those young barbarians we once were, blinded by our faith in that near horizon. One vital element will always be missing when we ape them: knowing how to enjoy it. That's what will give us away . . .'

I plunge into the network of little streets. Suddenly, a burst from a pneumatic drill just round the corner rattles out. My body reacts more swiftly than my mind, which is on its way back to civilization. It shudders as I swiftly repress the impulse to hurl myself to the ground, to lie flat, my brow hard against the sand. As on the parched soil of Afghanistan. My fingers grow numb from the weight of a missing automatic rifle. We shall never be normal people . . .

I stare into the glittering darkness of a shop window, straightening my tie. I must leave you now. My school for apes awaits me. A major publishing house. My assumed persona is a stereotype, Russian émigré writer. My normal person's uniform.

The boys in the courtyard, our playmates, always teased you in the same manner.

'Hey, Rezinka,' one of them would shout. Rezinka (India rubber), from Zinger, was your nickname. 'This is how your dad looks, right?'

He would suck in his cheeks and roll his eyes upwards, in imitation of a living corpse. You would hurl yourself at him with clenched fists, but rather half-heartedly. The joke had been repeated too often and now only provoked a few idle guffaws.

After all it was very difficult to imitate Yasha, your father. From the moment when he had been lifted out of a mountain of frozen bodies at a camp in liberated Poland he had changed little. He used to say it himself, with a smile. 'I never get any older. I'm just like I was at sixteen.'

His eyes were deeply sunken in gaping sockets. As if somebody had taken this head, resolved on demolishing it, and thrust his thumbs into them, embedding the eyes in the brain. His vast cranium, because of its waxen pallor, seemed to be made up of fragile planes that intersected almost geometrically. He had no teeth left and smiled with tightly clenched lips, stretching them in a rather painful grimace. It was really hard to mimic him.

When they had it in for me it was much simpler. Somebody would go down on his knees and shuffle forwards, puffing and blowing and waving his arms in comic despair.

'Hey, Kim,' he would cry, making mincemeat of my surname. 'This is your dad going to catch a train, right?'

But when all's said and done these jests were not cruel. They arose from boredom between marches. For the people in our three buildings had long since ceased to be surprised at seeing Yasha and my father crossing the courtyard in the summer dusk. From a distance you would have said it was a single man moving towards the main entrance with nimble steps . . .

The triangle formed by the three red brick structures contained a universe that was known to us down to the smallest clod of earth. Parallel with the walls of the buildings, and still following the same triangular formation, enormous poplar trees towered up, taller than the roofs. In June their feathery seeds transformed the courtyard into a winter landscape. People spat and sneezed the whole time and housewives cursed as they fished the fluffy lumps out of their bortsch.

At the base of the trees, beyond a fence of rotten timbers, there stretched impenetrable thickets made up of jasmine and lilac bushes and flowers with giant stems that were known as 'balls of gold'. In little enclaves, half hidden by this abundant vegetation, there were several benches, including Yasha's.

At the centre of the courtyard stood the dominoes players' table. Around it there were more trees, which were younger and seemed somehow closer to us, for we had watched them being planted. We were vaguely proud of knowing that we went further back in time than something in this courtyard . . .

The table, made from thick planks of knotty oak, presented a surface that was the first in springtime to shed its layer of snow, being the most exposed to the sun. It was an intense delight on a dazzling day in March to sit down there, to take a magnifying glass out of your pocket – a real treasure! – and mark your initials on the still damp timber. The fine bluish wisp of smoke tickled the nostrils and mingled with the snowy chill, before vanishing into the sunlit air . . .

In summer a regular routine was resumed. On warm evenings the table disappeared behind the backs of men in shirt-sleeves or jerseys. They grasped the slippery tiles in rough palms, made clumsy by the lumps of steel they handled all day, or by wrestling with the steering wheels of their heavy lorries. As soon as they began to slam down their pieces with a deafening din the communal symphony of the courtyard found its tempo. On a bench beside each main entrance a row of *babushkas* chattered away, attentive to the most minor occurrence in the courtyard. The open windows spilled out their buzz and with it came the sweetish, soapy smell of big washdays. The old swing groaned out its melancholy music. The shouts of invisible children pealed forth from among the bushes.

And like an absolutely essential note amid this

gentle evening cacophony, my mother's voice could be heard: 'Yasha!'

What did they talk about, those two men, sitting in their enclave amid the rampant clumps of dahlias and jasmine? It was of little interest to us, taken up as we were with the giddy round of our marching and our games. One day as I lingered near them, I heard a scrap of their conversation. It was nothing more, it seemed to me, than a slow recital of the names of towns. Polish, to judge by the sound of them. I already knew that my father had lost his legs in Poland and that Yasha had 'moved house', as he himself put it, three times from one camp to another. For them these Polish names, without further comment, were eloquent. A look they both understood, a tilt of the head, sufficed.

On another occasion I found myself behind them quite by chance. We were playing at war. Sent out as a scout, I was creeping along through the depths of the dense undergrowth, cocking my ear, my legs tingling with thrilling shivers, ready at the slightest danger to leap into a bounding retreat. Suddenly I heard their voices. They had that special clarity of words overheard unexpectedly. All that lay between me and the two men was a few dark jasmine branches. Intent on my secret mission, I would doubtless have continued on my way. But Yasha's voice, habitually calm, with a slightly ironic tone, this time had an unfamiliar vibrancy to it.

'The only snag they had with those damned lorries,' he was saying, 'was the business of unloading them. In fact, I think that's why they opted for the gas chambers. Because the idea of the lorries, slaughterhouses on wheels, was in many ways technically brilliant. They loaded people in directly at the doors to their huts. Once the engine started the exhaust fumes went straight through into the back. And when they arrived at the ovens everything was ready for burning. It only took a quarter of an hour. The length of the journey . . . To unload them there was an apparatus, you know, like a tipper . . . But it couldn't reach high enough inside the van on account of the corpses jammed against the roof. The mechanism kept breaking down. And besides, they needed men to do the unloading. One day I was detailed to do it. I was next to the van, I could hear the grinding of the mechanism inside the walls. There was an officer alongside it and a man in civilian clothes, probably an engineer. When they opened the doors the officer said to him: "If only we could achieve just another five degrees of height, I'm sure the load would slide out on its own." Yes, that was the precise word he used, "load". There was no hatred in his voice. And that was the most terrifying thing about it! Inside the van, where I climbed in with another prisoner, the jammed bodies had been crushed with the same absence of hatred. Mechanically. So we began unloading, slithering about on trickles of blood . . .'

Yasha fell silent. Leaning towards my father's cupped hands where a flame glimmered, he lit a cigarette.

As for me, I crawled backwards out of my hiding place, pushed aside a loose plank in the fence and stopped, unseeing, in front of the main entrance. Two of my comrades, from the enemy army that day, pounced on me, shouting in deafening unison: 'Hands up! You're dead! You're our prisoner!'

I acceded without offering the least resistance. With my arms in the air, and their wooden rifle sticking into my back, I advanced with a sleepwalker's tread. For the first time in my life I could not understand their glee . . .

Then a new marching season began that made me forget the conversation between the two men on their bench overgrown with greenery.

Once again a bright horizon hovered before our eyes in air that shimmered with the heat of summer. Once again, before passing through a village, our troop would carefully get in step, everyone tugging at the corners of his scarf.

You marched beside me and I would see your hands nervously poised above the drum, your drumsticks ready to shatter the sleepy tranquillity of the handful of *izbas*. While I chewed at lips atingle with pins and needles. When the sound finally exploded we were blind to everything. Everything but the brilliance of the flag above our heads and the far end of the country road trailing off into the sky. The troop's chief singer swallowed his saliva and yelled out in a piercing voice, with all the rest of us joining in:

We are the pioneers,
The workers' children we . . .
The age of radiant years
Is drawing ever nigh . . .
Always prepared are we,
Our motto bids us be . . .

It was only much later that other images we had unconsciously registered and preserved filtered through from this dazzling infatuation of our childhood. An old man walking along the road, stooping painfully to gather dusty sorrel leaves. The face of an old peasant woman who waved her hand feebly as we passed, smiling at us through her tears in a grimace ridged with wrinkles. Yes, it was only many years later that we sensed what it was those weary eyes could still recall. The countless ranks of soldiers who had once passed through that village before sinking without trace. They too had marched in step, stuck out their chests, concealed their tiredness. In those ranks there had been a brow, a pair of eyes, a shape that meant more to that peasant woman than life itself. They too had disappeared. Her old confused wits seemed to be rediscovering these features amid our own young shaven heads. This sweet lie sustained her . . .

But at the time all our eyes could see was the smile and the wave of the hand.

That evening a big wood fire burned at the centre of our camp. It was time now for other songs, slower, more reflective. One of them, even though we sang it every evening and knew the simple story by heart, always caused our eyes to gleam with somewhat moist reflections of the firelight. It was the one about the civil war. It had a deep, dreamy melancholy. We loved it all the more because it was indeed during the night that a young Red cavalryman had met his death, in a battle with the White Guards:

> He fell at the feet of his great black horse,
> Whispering, as his brown eyes closed:
> 'My steed, my friend, tell my true love
> I died keeping faith with the workers' cause . . .'

We could picture it all in such vivid detail! The 'broad Ukrainian steppe' mentioned in the song. The over-heated horse suddenly losing its master in full gallop. The few words whispered by a young horseman, his palm pressed against his bleeding breast, lying on the wet grass and turning his face hopelessly towards his companion's violet eyes.

What would we not have given, we too, at that moment, for the workers' cause! Could we picture a more beautiful death than to be stretched out on the steppe by night beneath the gaze of a faithful horse, expressive of a more than human compassion? Yes, to die grasping the hilt of one's sabre and contemplating the distress of a fiancée far away . . .

It was for the beauty of such a death that we loved 'the workers', in whose name one must sacrifice oneself, with a love that was almost holy. These workers bore no resemblance to the big men in jerseys, their faces ravaged by weariness, who played dominoes in the evening. No, those were too ordinary for our nocturnal reveries. They smoked, gripping their thick yellow cigarette stubs in fingers spotted with grease, swore and guffawed with guttural laughter. Their lives were too banal. Crammed into the beehives like the rest of us, they queued up for the communal bathroom like everyone else, and squeezed into the bus that took them to the factory.

The workers in our songs were different. They constituted a kind of superior tribe, untouched by the imperfections of our communal life. A worthy, austere and just people, for whom we must fight and suffer. It seemed to us that they were already waiting for us beyond the luminous line of the horizon that daily grew closer.

Our parents said little to us about the past. Perhaps they thought the past provided in songs and the stories in our training manuals was enough for us . . . Or did they simply want to spare us, well aware that in our country knowledge is a painful and often dangerous thing?

My father's life, or rather his youth, interested me a great deal. Like some seeker after treasure, I felt certain I could discover images in his past as a soldier comparable to those of the nocturnal battle in which the Red cavalryman met his death. A heroic hand-to-hand combat. A dazzling exploit. But his tales were always drily and disappointingly sober.

I then embarked, almost unconsciously, on constructing a kind of fresco, a mosaic of this youth that fascinated me. Day after day I added fragments from his stories, unguarded confidences, details that emerged by chance in his chats with my mother.

Indirectly and, indeed, without suspecting it, Yasha had helped me greatly in my long gathering of little shards for this mosaic. There was one thing Yasha wanted at all costs to avoid talking about in company: his own sufferings, life in the camps. If ever he had the feeling that this topic might be brought up, he would hasten to ask for a light, or, at dinners on high days and holidays, propose an amusing toast that made everyone laugh. Immediately afterwards, to change the subject once and for all, he would say to my father: 'Now then, Pyotr, why don't you tell us the rest of that story, you remember, when you were in Byelorussia? Last time you didn't finish it . . .'

For my mosaic I even used the odd remark that the dominoes players would call out to my father when he sat down to play with them. Even in these I found a handful of fragments that evoked his youth, the war. A few trifles that I could add to my summarily reconstructed mural.

One day you had asked me, with that spontaneous abruptness we were all marked with by life: 'So, your father, what did he do in the war?'

'How do you mean, "What?" He shot. He killed Germans,' I replied in a rather doubtful voice. 'He killed thousands and thousands of them . . .'

At the time I did not know much about it. Your revelation to me of my own ignorance may have been the starting point for my mosaic.

Now, all these years later, I can unveil it before your eyes (in 'Portland . . . Cleveland . . .'). As before, it is incomplete. But today we can be sure no more fragments will ever be added to its uneven surface . . .

Incomplete Mosaic of a Youth in the War

In his early days at the front it did not feel to Pyotr as if he was killing people. In his capacity as a sniper he had a very particular relationship with death . . .

The human figure in his sights that had to be immobilized had become familiar to him while still young. Like all his generation, living in 'the besieged fortress of socialism', he had learned to shoot very early, in the training circle of the 'Voroshilov marksmen'.

In the war a great distance always separated him from his living targets and that, too, seemed to soften the deaths he caused. The human figurines, over half a mile distant, looked very much like the plywood silhouettes he used to pepper with lead during the old days, in his training with the circle. Tiny dolls moving about beside papier mâché *izbas*. Jumping jacks whose very heedlessness was provocative.

He would take up a stance somewhere on high ground, seeking out shadow, thick foliage. Most of the time he went to work with the help of an observer. But on occasion he took up position on his own.

His secret vigil would then be steeped in perfect silence. His eye glued to the rifle's telescopic sight kept watch on a distant scene. The air between the barrel and the target became more and more dense, tangible. Pyotr felt his own breath dissolving into this space that was concentrated by the sharpness of his gaze.

At the other end of this distance a village, occupied by the Germans, was living out its strange wartime routine. Jolting motorcycles with sidecars swept past the big *izba* where the staff headquarters was located.

A broad black car swayed along the rutted road. The door to the *izba* opened, people went in and out, paused on the front steps. They shook hands, saluted, talked. All this – as if in the glaucous transparency of an aquarium – was encrusted in the compact silence of the eyepiece.

Pyotr saw an old woman walking along beside a hedge with a furtive gait, crossing the road. A terrified chicken just managed to escape the wheels of the black car. A pot with a pale flower in it drowsed behind a murky windowpane.

The telescopic sight's attentive circle slid across this noiseless space and began to focus on human figures . . . Over there a soldier, a tall gangling fellow, is walking towards a well, carrying two empty buckets. The wind adjustment graduations in the telescopic sight follow him for a moment, then let him go; he would be too easy a prey. He is still in the field of vision, this great hulk. This is a good sign as well: as long as he is there one can be sure there have been no troop movements.

The watery circle slides towards the open window of the *izba*. A young officer sits writing by the window, another is seated beside him and seems to be talking to an invisible interlocutor. Which one of the two? No, it is better to wait a bit. If death comes in through a narrow window it shows too clearly the place where the sniper is hiding. Wait.

The young officer puts his papers into a briefcase,

vanishes, reappears on the front steps, runs briskly down them, and walks towards a motorcycle that is waiting for him in the courtyard. The soldier jerks upright on his saddle, as he starts the engine. The officer settles into the sidecar and at the same moment, as if he had sunk into a deep reverie, he lets his chin fall on his chest. With the backfiring of the engine the soldier has noticed nothing.

The empty cartridge case flies out, the new cartridge slides into place. Boring a hole in the tranquil summer's day, the silent circle approaches the *izba* once more.

The two conversationalists appear on the steps. One of them takes out a cigar case, the other rummages in his pocket. Yes, that must be it, the lighter has been left indoors. He goes to look for it . . . The vital thing now is to stay awake!

The officer who has just opened the cigar case suddenly flings it away, as if in disgust, grasps the handrail and crumples up. As his companion comes out, fiddling with the lighter, he has time to see the cigarettes scattered before collapsing in the doorway, with his head thrown back.

Now every second counted. To put a cover over the telescopic sight, gather up the three cartridge cases and, alternating between short bursts of running and frozen pauses, to reach the nearest thicket.

Around the staff headquarters the people were already in turmoil. They pointed in the direction of the copse Pyotr had just left. Yes, they had guessed: a sniper. Raising a cloud of dust, the motorcycle combination returned towards the front steps with its dead passenger. The silence was broken by the furious barking of dogs.

Pyotr knew that he would get away. He knew that the soldiers flung towards the copse in pursuit of him would flounder about for a good ten minutes in a marshy meadow. He had noticed it the previous day when he was crawling along choosing his position. He knew that when they were finally close to the copse they would start raking the thick foliage of a great oak tree with bursts of fire. But Pyotr had never gone anywhere near this tree. For he knew the time-honoured rule that regularly saved his life: when choosing a place to shoot from, seek out the best location, a well-protected spot on high ground – now move a good distance away from it and select another, much less suitable. Then you may have a chance of surviving.

He returned to his regiment that evening, spoke to the commandant and took his rest. Before going to bed he cut three fine notches on the butt of his rifle.

Right from the start he had viewed the war through the hazy transparency of the telescopic sight. By dint of this his right eyebrow had become arched, as if expressing permanent amazement . . . As for the notches on the butt – there were already almost a hundred.

It was in Byelorussia that the deaths of the people who were swallowed up in the watery glass of his telescopic sight one day became real to Pyotr.

His position, this time, was a dream: a steep riverbank, a tangle of willow groves, and, just beyond that, the forest. A little town occupied by the Germans offered itself to view as if spread out on the palm of a hand. Low houses, wide streets. It lay in a single field of fire from one end to the other.

'We've got a real rest cure, here,' Pyotr said to himself.

He took up position, created a shelter in the fork of a tree, beat down a pathway for his withdrawal, studied the air currents, allowed for the pitfall presented by the river. Rivers or ravines always deceive marksmen, they cause distances to vanish and seem to bring targets closer. Finally, taking his time, he began to explore this silent town, peopled with grey military figures.

The first day he made two notches on the rifle butt; the second, three. 'It's like a fairground shooting booth,' he said to himself. He even killed a soldier whom, at first, he did not want to touch. The man was in the middle of the courtyard, stretched out full length, and playing the mouth organ. He looked as if he were deliberately offering himself to the bullet.

The next day the Germans were wary. At the main crossroads in the town, where Pyotr had killed two officers, a plywood screen had been erected. Pyotr could no longer see people crossing the road, and the cars and motorcycles also went past under the shelter of this panel. 'Who cares,' he chuckled. 'You can't all hide behind the screen,' and he began to study the streets.

Almost at once he spotted an entire council of war beneath a broad mulberry tree in one of the courtyards. At a garden table two officers sat with their backs to him. Another stood facing them, leaning against the trunk of the tree. There were papers spread out on the table top.

'Those must be maps,' thought Pyotr.

His eye slid first over the backs of the seated men, then moved onto the figure of the one standing up. Yes. There. Just below the glittering metallic eagle on his chest.

Slowly Pyotr squeezed the trigger. The officer remained motionless. The two others did not move either.

'Hell's bells!' breathed Pyotr, taken aback. 'I've been and gone and missed him!'

He reloaded, aimed again – at the eagle – fired. The officer did not flinch.

Dumbfounded, Pyotr narrowed his eyes and uttered a cry of surprise. A little trickle of dust was spilling out of the officer's chest.

'I don't believe it!' murmured Pyotr. 'They must have . . .'

He had no time to formulate his thought, understood everything, hurled himself down from his tree fork to the ground, and rolled towards the pathway through the willow groves he had made two days before.

Under a hail of machinegun fire his shelter was already being transformed into a whirlwind of mutilated foliage.

This crackling was accompanied by another noise, closer, louder – someone was firing at him with a submachine-gun. Pyotr rolled some more. Clinging to life, his body seemed to ricochet off the uneven ground. When he was able to get up he felt a strange numbness where his right foot should be. As if his boot were swathed in a great cushion.

That evening the medical orderly extracted a submachine-gun bullet from his foot. Pyotr cleaned the mud-spattered telescopic sight, then reached from habit for a penknife to carve some notches and spat with vexation at the recollection of the dummy officer filled with sand.

'I fell for that like some kid wet behind the ears,' he repeated to himself, unable to sleep, tormented by rage and burning twinges from his foot. Then in the night he mastered his pain and calmed down.

'Lucky to be alive,' he reflected, his gaze lost in the warm, dark rectangle of the half-open window. The wind scattered this blackness with occasional drops of hesitant rain. And Pyotr again recalled the officer at the foot of the tree, with a little haze of dust escaping from his tunic . . .

Suddenly a dazzlingly simple notion occurred to him. He pictured all the bullets he had despatched, not into statues of sand but into living people. Before then he had never given it a thought . . .

As a child I was vaguely disappointed at not having come across that Red cavalryman again in my own father's story. Other people found it hard to understand what he was driving at when he talked about his thoughts that night after he was wounded.

Only Yasha took a serious interest in the end of the story. He would press the point: 'And after that did you go on shooting them down, just as before?'

'After that I stopped making notches . . .' my father replied.

He had lost his legs on the German-Polish border: on returning from one of his missions he had come under fire from an artillery bombardment by our own army. They were preparing an offensive along a whole front and evidently could not anticipate the position of one sniper, a certain Pyotr Yevdokimov . . .

The fact that he had been wounded not by the Germans, but by our own artillery, was subsequently a source of considerable complications for my father. They would not even recognize this injury as a war wound. So he had not been allocated the invalid car that others had received. It was Yasha who, by moving heaven and earth, much later managed to ensure that he obtained one . . .

In our courtyard there were two quite special locations that, each in its own way, shaped the topography of our young years.

First of all there was the 'Pit'. An almost mythical place and as much a part of our vision of the world as the clouds, the moon and the sun. It was a kind of pool with high banks covered in plants that did not grow anywhere else. Little flowers, with the bluish luminosity of neon, perched on sticky, fleshy stems. The surface of this little crater was covered in duckweed and it was surrounded by the inevitable poplar trees. It even seemed to us that the leaves of these poplars rustled in a quite special way and cast shadows of a different consistency.

What lay at the bottom of the Pit? Why had it not been filled in? For us these questions were as mysterious as the origins of the world. We would throw stones into it, we would test its muddy depths with poles, but the Pit guarded its secret well.

Apparently the only person who knew anything more about it was Zakharovna, an old woman with sharp little eyes half hidden by a headscarf. One of the three red brick buildings had been erected where her *izba* once stood. She certainly knew the history of the Pit. But Zakharovna, it was common knowledge, was becoming daily more unhinged. And whenever anybody questioned her on the subject she would give a sly, mad smile and reply with some quite unlikely phrase: 'So then? Did you sin together and confess separate?'

And she would begin to chuckle. People shrugged their shoulders. 'When you're mad, you're mad . . .'

Throughout the winter, however, that is for a good half of the year, the Pit lost its daunting appearance. Its surface froze over and became transformed into an excellent skating rink.

In summer it had its uses too. Sometimes a brawl erupted at the dominoes table. Had someone cheated? Had there been an argument? The men would get up, hurl the dominoes to the ground, and start shoving and grappling with one another. Finally one of them would utter the ritual challenge: 'Right. I'll see you round the back of the Pit. I'll make you drink from it, you silly sod!'

The word 'Pit' was a signal to the whole courtyard. The children broke off their games. The rows of *babushkas* on their benches became agitated. Women appeared at the open windows and filled the courtyard with shrill cries, calling to their husbands.

'Lyosha!'

'Sergey!'

'Vanya!'

Everyone understood that if the word 'Pit' had been uttered things were getting serious.

At that moment Yasha often appeared at the table with my father. He would set him down on the bench and say in a calm voice that mysteriously cut through the uproar of the argument: 'Right, that's enough, boys. Let's have another game now. I bet you won't be a match for Pyotr and myself.'

Fretting and fuming, the men picked up the dominoes. It was one of the rare occasions when those two would play together.

The second location was called the 'Gap'.

Our three buildings were situated at the edge of the little town of Sestrovsk. They faced inwards onto the courtyard, and seemed to proclaim their own autonomy. There was this town and its huge factory with black chimneys, a cinema, a station. There was Leningrad, misty and alluring, half an hour away by train. But the courtyard clung jealously to its independence. The Gap contributed greatly to this. It was one of the apexes of our triangular courtyard, an apex facing not towards the town but towards open waste ground.

The other two apexes had long since been cluttered up with grey wooden sheds and woodpiles. They were redolent, especially in winter, of damp bark and rabbit hutches. In these cramped shacks the inhabitants of the three buildings kept their tools, reared rabbits and chickens and, above all, accumulated unbelievable old junk which, they thought, could not fail to come in handy one day. From time to time it would transpire that one of the padlocks on one of the doors had been forced. The affair would set the whole courtyard in uproar. People would imagine the most dramatic scenarios. They would work out the likely hour of the break-in. They would point a finger at the guilty ones – who could only be people from outside, of course. Often, moreover, the crime was confined to the breaking of an old padlock – the contents of the shack being touchingly useless.

The third apex of the courtyard, the Gap, was beyond these smells and this mundane turbulence. It faced north west and at times when there were cold sunsets veritable palaces of cloud arose there. The summer evenings were light and long and the marbled and vaporous sumptuousness of the northern sky did not fade away. It remained frozen there, above the three red brick buildings, above the dominoes table, above the Pit.

The sky no longer floated along, all flat, parallel to the earth. It reared up vertically. Within this white and pink mass columns arose, gothic arches took shape, spires thrust upwards. The mauve light reflected from this beauty coloured the faces of the players, the pages of a large book on Yasha's knees, the pillowcases and sheets that a woman was hanging up on lines stretched beside the jasmine bushes.

Lying on the grass, we stared silently at this vertical sky, not knowing what to make of its aerial architecture. We knew that somewhere beyond the open ground, only a few dozen miles away, lay the sea. A sea that led to unknown lands, all those Englands and Americas. We knew their cruel and unjust existence was drawing to a close, and their inhabitants would soon be joining us on our march towards the radiant horizon. But as we lay beneath these cloudy castles not even these thoughts touched us. For a moment the marching had stopped, the country roads still rang with the echo of our songs. We marked a pause.

The dominoes clattered, plates and dishes rattled together in busy kitchens and something arose above the Gap for which we had no name but which nevertheless made us happy.

They had met on the third anniversary of the Victory.

Pyotr had long since settled down into his role as a disabled man. He had come to accept it. He moved around on a kind of trolley he had made for himself, a chest mounted on four big wheels, with ball bearings.

On tarmac roads it moved well, he overtook passers-by, but on the earth, especially in spring and autumn, he suffered as if on a treadmill, twisting and turning in his crate, swearing and thrusting his two sticks into the ground. In winter he did not go out at all, spending whole days in the *izba* belonging to Zakharovna, who let half a room to him.

On that day in May he got up, splashed his face from the bowl that Zakharovna placed every morning next to the curtain marking off his corner, shaved and combed his hair with particular care. He took his greatcoat off the mattress, where it served him as a blanket. He was afraid the morning might be chilly. Then, climbing onto a piece of hessian, he slid across the floor towards the exit, towards his crate on wheels.

The weather was mild. He folded up his greatcoat, and laid it in the bottom of the crate. That was certainly more comfortable. The earth, still soft and damp, gave way under his efforts, the wheels with their ball bearings got stuck but today this did not seem to trouble Pyotr unduly. He moved on towards the tarmac road, inhaled the bitter scent of the poplar shoots and even softly whistled a tune recalled from the war.

An hour later he was at his usual spot in front of the left wing of the railway station, beside the staircase used by passengers coming into the town.

When the muffled voice from the loudspeaker announced the arrival of the train from Leningrad Pyotr sat up in his seat and moulded his features into an expression that was both mournful and submissive.

The passers-by gave freely. The spring air and the public holiday made them generous. Some of them bent down a little to put money in his palm, others, in a hurry, tossed their roubles into the crate . . .

Pyotr counted his take in the little dusty garden next to the station. Before setting off again he ate the slice of bread he had put in the pocket of his greatcoat that morning. After three years he knew the route by heart: the station, a loaf of bread at the baker's, a bottle in a booth by the market entrance.

Almost all of his disability pension went to Zakharovna. The money he collected at the bottom of his crate was transformed into long evenings beside the open window when his mind slowly became clouded, and the outlines of the houses melted into the distance. His body would melt too, like candle wax. He could be kneaded at will, moulded into any shape you chose. And all the 'if onlys' that had tormented him over the years became less and less impossible . . .

Pyotr accelerated spiritedly and headed for the market stall at full tilt, with ball bearings rattling. It was a kind of kiosk attached to the wall, with a little window too high for him, through which the goods were served. He began knocking on the side of it.

'Mila!' he called up from below. 'Are you asleep or what? Let's have two half litres!'

Mila, a buxom market woman, who generally recognized the rattling of his cart from a long way off, made no reply.

Pyotr could not see the window very well and the whole front of the stall was encumbered with tins of food, packets of tea and bottles.

'Come on, wakey, wakey, you great fat lump!' he cried angrily, drumming even more fiercely on the edge of the window.

Suddenly he heard a voice above him.

'What is it you want?'

He shifted in his crate, turned round. The side door to the stall was open. A young woman stood in front of him with her hand on the handle.

'Where's Mila?' he demanded rather brusquely.

'She's got the day off,' replied the young woman. 'I'm filling in for her.'

'Ah, I see . . . the day off,' Pyotr repeated and fell silent.

She was silent as well, her hand still on the handle. She was not beautiful, only young. Her dull hair gathered into a bunch at the back of her neck, her eyes grey, her face plain, little used to smiling.

But he, on the other hand, had a rather splendid look about him. He was boldly upright on his folded greatcoat, one fist on his hip, his medals pinned to his combat uniform for the occasion. A little out of breath from his efforts, he was breathing deeply. His face was young, animated by his haste. His eyes dark, with a hint of bitter madness in his look. A lock of fair, curly hair hung over his brow. He was handsome. If only . . . If only . . .

'What is it you want?' she asked again, trying to smile at him.

'A packet of Belomor,' he said, after a brief hesitation.

Without going into her kiosk, she first took the cigarettes from the display through the open door, then the note he offered her.

Pyotr tossed the packet into the crate, gripped his

sticks and began thrusting furiously against the ground. Faster, faster! He was almost fleeing. The sand grated under the wheels, the pavement clattered. On the corner of the street he turned and saw her, still standing upright at the open door.

He bought his two bottles at the other end of the town. At home he found a piece of fish pâté on the stool where Zakharovna used to leave the bowl in the morning. A holiday treat.

He was lying on his spring mattress, beneath the open window. The bottle and the glass close to hand. Vague sounds and barely perceptible scents drifted in from outside, impinging on his slow, confused thoughts. He was already moulding himself, adding into this malleable clay something of the gilded clouds at the end of the day, a handful of pre-war days, the avenues that once opened up so willingly before you. Now he mixed in a timid echo of the smile the young woman at the market stall had given him. Catching his eye, a dazzling beam of coppery light slipped onto the floor, and laid to rest the residue of incredulity within him.

When the young market girl appeared behind his curtain, accompanied by whispering from Zakharovna, Pyotr did not even stir. Why spoil the stately course of his dreams? She stopped, irresolute, holding back the flap of the curtain. The dazzling sunbeam slid over to her feet. He looked at her from his blissful fog and still did not stir.

'I forgot to give you your change,' she softly said at last and put down a crumpled note and several coins on a corner of the stool.

Pyotr closed his eyes.

Almost everything about my mother's childhood was unknown to me.

One day, when the *babushkas* were chatting, I overheard a sigh and a remark mentioning my mother's name.

'Who? Lyuba? Yevdokimova? Well, let me tell you. What she went through as a girl I wouldn't wish on my worst enemy . . .'

The phrase stuck in my mind. I spent a long time wondering what this fearful thing might be that you wouldn't even wish upon an enemy.

The rare occasions when my mother talked to me about her childhood years coincided in my memory with Sunday evenings in winter; it was the day she did her ironing.

From the courtyard she would bring in an enormous armful of laundry covered in hoar-frost and put it down on the chest. All the petrified sheets, shirts with sleeves as hard as cardboard and rigid socks, bent in half, would glitter with a thousand crystals beneath the dull light of the electric bulb. And what the angular pile gave off, above all, was the rough, fresh smell of winter. The frozen heap seemed to be breathing.

My mother took off her coat, and seated herself, to give the laundry time to 'settle down', as she put it. I would perch with my bowl of warm milk at the corner of the table. Outside the window the dusk was already glowing blue. It was at such times that she began to talk, her big red hands relaxed on her knees, her gaze lost in the blue as it grew slowly deeper outside the window. For me her stories were always associated with that aromatic heap on the chest, the blissful relaxation of that woman with her cold, red hands.

And if you came to see me at that moment, she would get up and, without interrupting her story, still relaxed and dreamy, would pour you a bowl of milk. And we would listen together.

Tale with the Smell of Frozen Laundry, One Sunday over the Ironing

I shall call her Lyuba, which is what everyone in the courtyard called her. What the *babushkas* called her, who would not have wished the girlhood she had on their worst enemy.

It seemed to Lyuba as if she had never seen her father in his indoor clothes. He always had his supple leather shoulder belt slung about him, and wore his high black boots. In the days of the harshest purges ('when Yezhov was in charge,' as my mother used to say, so as to avoid naming Stalin in front of us) for weeks at a time her father used to go to bed without undressing. Every night he knew they could come searching for him at any moment and take him away.

By the end of 1939 he believed he could begin to breathe again. Thinking the worst was over, he even allowed himself to relax a little. For the New Year he dressed up as Father Christmas, especially for her, his daughter. He rigged himself out with a cotton wool beard and her only memory of him was this unrecognizable face, the conventional face of Father Christmas. Unconsciously, she spent the rest of her life trying to picture the features, the look, the smile that lay beneath this crude disguise . . .

After New Year's Day, for the winter holidays, Lyuba went with her mother to the country.

In the Siberian *izba*, redolent of cedar and birch logs, the course of life was quite different. Here, for example, even the milk was transported to the village in quite another way. In the resonant cold of the morning the delicate music of sleigh bells would arise. They would lift up their heads from their teacups and cock an ear. Soon they could hear the crunching of runners, the harsh clatter of hooves. They stood up and put on their sheepskin coats.

A horse had come to a stop in the yard, all white and encrusted with hoar-frost. Glebych, an old man with a rubicund face, swung himself heavily down from the sledge. When he saw them descending the front steps he would bend down, withdraw a coarse grey cloth from the sledge and spread it out. Lyuba's eyes opened wide. In his big fur mittens Glebych was holding a broad disc of frozen milk that glistened in the morning sun. Carefully he laid it on the embroidered napkin that her mother held out to him.

On the ribbed surface of the crystalline disc Lyuba sometimes discovered a wisp of straw stuck to it or an ear of corn. Sometimes even a cornflower. . . . But her greatest delight was secretly to go up to the big frozen block, lick it right in the middle, and feel the breath of an exhilarating chill on her face!

Did they love one another, Lyuba and Pyotr? When I was a child the question never occurred to me. Everything seemed natural to me. I simply could not imagine my father being any different, or my mother experiencing any regrets at having such a husband, at knowing him to be irremediably as he was.

Everything in our lives seemed natural to us. The doors to our flats that were never locked at night – like the burrows in an anthill. And your father marking homework on the windowsill. He taught mathematics at the school . . . Nor were we surprised by your mother's activities in the evenings. She wrote letters. Scores of letters. To ministries, to the Central Committee, to the local soviets. In them she always made the same request: that in a little garden in Leningrad a monument should be erected in memory of the victims of the siege. In reply she always received the same refusals that bore the hallmarks of administrative politeness, or else simply silence. 'At the very least a marble plaque on the wall!' she would beg. 'There is no provision for this in the five-year plan for the social development of the area,' they would reply. She persevered, for she bore within her the harrowing memory of all the deaths she had witnessed as a child in the city under siege. She would be writing. . . . Your father would be making marks in red ink beside countless columns of figures . . . And you would get up, turn down the corner of a page and come along to see us.

Twice in succession, first in your flat and then in ours, which was strictly identical, you had to make your way through a continuous human bustle. In the communal corridor children bowled along on their little bicycles. A man was painting a door. A woman carrying an enormous basin of boiling water emerged from the kitchen and, with a resounding 'whoosh', emptied the contents into the bathtub full of washing. The corridor filled with hot steam and smells of laundry.

'Yegorych! Have you gone to sleep in there?' somebody demanded, rattling the lavatory door handle.

'Katya!' a woman's voice cut through the steam. 'Off to bed, quickly!'

In the kitchen they were furiously scouring huge black cast-iron frying pans. And the music from a record player lulled us all with nostalgia for remote islands:

> When I left for Havana, that land of blue,
> My sorrow was known, my love, only to you . . .

Inside our door it all started up again: the hubbub, the bustle, a restless music that seemed to insinuate itself among the busy women, seeking out a space where it could flow in all tranquillity.

We were never surprised when you came into our room without knocking and sat down beside me. My mother would get up, pour you some milk and continue with her story.

A ringing noise responded to her words. It came from a tiny cubby-hole. There my father carried out his work as a cobbler.

After their marriage my mother had had this idea: what more sedentary job could one think of than that of a cobbler? It was she who had obtained the authorization from the soviet, she who had procured all the necessary tools. When my father moved from Zakharovna's *izba* into this communal flat, they set up his tiny workshop in a lumber room. Having spent his youth in the country he had hands that could endow any object with life. He knew how to make them all obedient, useful.

'Cobbler? Why not?' he had replied to my mother's suggestion. 'Only we'll have to find some lasts – you know, those cast-iron feet . . .'

There was never any shortage of customers. Shoes were unobtainable or too costly. So people went on repairing them until they crumbled into dust. A whole row of shoes, boots and bootees was laid out along the wall. Amid their shrivelled wrinkles each pair displayed its ailments: soles with toothy grins, twisted heels, dents. Sometimes there were so many of them that the queue stretched out over the threshold of the workshop and lined up along the wall of our room. At mealtimes we might glance at it and make comments.

'Look, Zoïka's broken her heel again! That woman thinks of nothing but putting herself about on the dance floor . . . Heavens! Yegorych is getting ready for winter: he's brought in his big walking boots. He looks ahead, that fellow . . .'

Another queue, not so long, was formed by the repaired shoes. With their thick new soles they had a robust and resolute look.

It was thanks to this row of footwear awaiting their owners that, for the first time in my life, in a bizarre and rather comic fashion, I became aware of the complexity and fragility of the world beyond the triangle of our courtyard . . .

One day I noticed a pair of men's shoes in the line-up that looked a good deal more elegant than their solid neighbours. You could still see the trace of a gilded stamp inside them. The laces were unusually round and woven. I was very eager to see the stranger who came in to collect them. But he was a long time coming. His shoes were overtaken by the others, relegated to a corner. My father, mainly out of regard for their tarnished elegance, polished them a little from time to time. Still the owner did not come. He would never come. And for the first time I had a sense of the troubling vastness of cities, spaces where a man could go under, vanish just like that, leaving his shoes in a little lumber room in an unknown communal flat . . .

My father used to nail little steel tips in the shape of a crescent moon onto the heels of the shoes. On pavements they made a ringing, almost melodious noise. Thanks to this noise the inhabitants of our courtyard could recognize one another in the streets of Leningrad when they went there on occasion to buy provisions. Suddenly amid the ordinary footsteps on the Nevsky Prospekt we would hear this inimitable chinking sound, we would turn, lift up our hands to heaven and exclaim: 'Well I never! Those are some of our neighbours from Sestrovsk!'

And we would embrace as if we had not seen one another for years . . .

. . . My mother would finish the ironing and you

would get up, wish us good night and leave the room. I would retire behind the plywood partition, in the corner where my narrow bed was located. Over it, hanging from a nail, was my bugle. I could hear my mother's muffled voice as she stopped on the threshold of the lumber room, talking to my father. I could picture him clearly – seated on a stool wedged against the wall, a thick needle thrust into the big knot at the end of one trouser leg, a shoe mounted on a last.

When I came out from my corner one evening I saw my mother standing in the doorway of the little cubby-hole. She was silent and unmoving, staring fixedly at the light bulb's yellow halo. My father had his head resting against her breast in a posture of silent repose I had never seen him in before. His eyes were closed . . . Hearing my footsteps they bestirred themselves.

'Go to bed, Pyetya,' my mother said to him softly. 'You can finish it tomorrow.'

'One more nail,' he replied with a smile.

My father was a man of the soil. He had always detested hunting, having one day seen a huntsman advancing on a wounded hare to finish it off. He had heard the little animal's terrible cry, seen its eyes filled with real tears . . . But we lived in a 'besieged fortress of socialism' and every citizen needed to be able to shoot accurately.

What he really missed was no longer being able to work with a scythe. He often spoke to us about those mornings in the meadows, the chill grass falling beneath the blade in a fan silvered with dew. He would often repeat a rhyme, like a distant echo of those mornings that would never return:

> Cut, cut, my bonny scythe
> While the dew still shines,
> When it's gone,
> We'll go home.

It was for that reason that no one had ever called him Cobbler. Everyone understood that he was made for something else . . .

There was one quite extraordinary summer in the life of the courtyard, in our own lives. Filled from start to finish with remarkable events.

It all began one afternoon in May. Yasha burst into our room, waving a typed sheet of paper above his head and exclaimed: 'Pyotr, this is it! We've won . . . Your car: you're going to get it! I've beaten them, those idiots . . .'

And indeed two days later all the inhabitants came out into the courtyard to see my father, solemn and radiant, making a circuit of it at the steering wheel of a little *invalidka*. Beside him sat Yasha.

The tiny car looked like a dog kennel: it had only two seats and backfired deafeningly. But it was a pretty, dark cherry colour and, what is more, it was the only car in the courtyard! That same evening Yasha knocked down the partition between our two sheds and threw out all the old junk. The first car acquired the first garage.

My father would have found it hard to conceal his gratitude.

'Listen, Yasha, you've been lugging me around for long enough. Now I'm going to take you to school every morning! Agreed?'

Yasha, who used to reach his place of work in ten minutes via short cuts, tried to dodge this generous offer. But above all he did not want to disappoint my father.

The next day they set off together, following the main street of the town. It must have felt odd to my father to be travelling down roads where previously he had plodded along with his two sticks, seated in a jolting crate . . . Already he was brimming with plans for long journeys. To Leningrad, for example, or even to Moscow, why not . . .

Then one evening all eyes were directed towards the sky as it slowly filled with stars. The first sputnik had just been launched! It was Yasha who gave us commentaries. These turned the life of the courtyard upside down for several weeks, even distracting the dominoes players from their favourite activity.

'There is quite a brief moment,' he told us, 'when it's possible to see it with the naked eye. When the sun has set, and the sky grows dark, but the sun has not yet sunk too far below the line of the horizon. That's when you can make out the sputnik against the background of the sky, lit by the sun's rays, even though the sun itself is hidden . . .'

How tensely we awaited that fleeting moment! Above the Gap the cloud castles slowly darkened, travelling towards the Baltic. The first stars trembled. And we, with our heads tilted back, scanned the sky. From time to time someone would utter a cry: 'Over there, over there! I can see it!' and point an index finger towards a star that seemed to be moving. Others would look in that direction and discover his mistake. People would laugh: 'Go to bed, astronomer! Put your specs on, Copernicus!'

At all events, during the course of that summer everyone claimed to have seen the sputnik at least once. This vigil under the evening sky, this roaming among the first stars imported a special element of calm into the communal turbulence of the three buildings.

Our ardent marching towards the promise of the horizon was marked that year by a yet more vibrant enthusiasm. As if the whole world had heard the bugle's joyful call and the tattoo on the drum.

One day, when a halt was called, I saw you looking at a map spread out on the grass. You were pointing a finger at a little oblong island lost in the dark blue of the ocean: 'This is only a first spark. The whole of America will catch fire! Just think, soon it'll be called the Soviet Socialist Republic of America!'

But for the moment the little oblong island, which for us had no other name but the Isle of Freedom, looked like a tiny fish ready to be swallowed up in the gaping maw of the Gulf of Mexico. And imperialist Florida loomed over it like a menacing fang.

Our rallying call had been heard. Already Africa was shaking the chains of slavery, as our instructor used to put it.

'You must prepare to defend all peoples in love with liberty against the tyranny of American imperialism,' he would add, looking us each in the eye one by one.

So the song we sang most often that summer chimed well with the struggle we looked forward to, burning with impatience:

> From Moscow to far Britain's shores
> The Red Army will conquer all . . .

You used to dream of learning 'the African language'. For this would make our struggle all the more effective. I was preparing for it differently: I took off my sandals and marched barefoot over the pine needles, the stony ground, the hot sand . . . And when, after a march, we happened to hear in the courtyard the dreamy nostalgia of the record player singing 'Havana, that land of blue', we shrugged our shoulders indignantly. How could anyone talk of this 'land of blue' as long as the fang of Florida threatened the Isle of Freedom?

All in all, we were bursting with naïve and spontaneous good will; we felt a need to help, to rescue, to show ourselves to be generous. An impulse quite natural and proportional to the extreme poverty in which we lived. This impulse could be manipulated, directed towards a specific goal. The mechanism for this manipulation had long since been tried and tested. But how could we know that?

At night we sometimes mounted guard together at camp. First of all we took several turns among the sleeping tents, then we stoked up the fire and became absorbed in our silent occupations. Lacking a textbook of the African language, you were learning the Morse alphabet. I was tending the soles of my feet, removing splinters and applying plantain leaves to the scratches.

Finally, to keep ourselves awake, we would both take up our instruments and embark on a silent duet. Without putting the bugle to my lips I would blow into it softly. And a sound could be heard, barely audible, yet quite profound and subtle. As if, at the end of the world a weary saxophone player were pouring out a lethargic and interminable blues into the night air. You caressed the skin of your drum with your fingers and this dry friction kept time with the saxophone player's weary melody. Thus we lived out the rhythm of a night whose existence we sensed unconsciously. We said nothing to one another in those moments. We stared at the glowing embers and with half-closed eyes focused on the modulations of the unknown music that was being born within us . . .

Yes, that summer brought us many extraordinary things. Even the habits of the dominoes players changed. We noticed now that their pieces would often be abandoned in a useless pile. And they talked. They argued hard. The names of Stalin, Khrushchev, Zhukov and Castro came hurtling out and landed with as much clatter as their dominoes did in the old days.

'He killed twenty million!'

'He won the war!'

'Without Zhukov he wouldn't have won anything!'

'What about the camps!'

'And the corn!'

'And law and order!'

The pitch rose. The voices grew heated.

'Listen! I had four years in the trenches, in the front line! And you don't even know which end to load a rifle!'

'Hang about, my brave lads! I finished the war in Berlin!'

'Ha ha, in Berlin . . . Yes. In the cookhouse, with your arse in the soup!'

Finally the word 'Pit' would interrupt the communal symphony of the evening.

'Listen, Pyotr, let's go over there,' Yasha would say to my father, who sat beside him in the recess. 'Let's have a game or two . . .'

During these long evenings the groans that came from the old swing were more languorous than ever. And we, wildly envious, watched the wide arc of the wooden plank. On its unstable surface, standing upright, with their hands gripping the ropes, they flew into the sky together, She and He. Lyoshka-the-Japanese, who was known by this name because of his slightly slanting eyes, and Zoïka, who used to bring her shoes with their broken heels to my father almost every week. Those two were the boldest and most reckless people in the whole courtyard. The *babushkas* grumbled about them on principle: 'I ask you, would any self-respecting girl fly like that with her skirt in the air? She looks more like a parachutist!'

But it was all in good part, without ill-feeling.

Zoïka hurled herself forward. The groaning rose to an intolerable pitch. The girl's hair, flung into the sky, blazed in the sinking sun. Fascinated, we contemplated her high heels as they dragged lightly against the plank, and risked coming unstuck altogether. Her long legs, too, exposed right up to dizzying limits. And her joyful eyes still dazzled by the sunlight that had already quit the courtyard.

Lyoshka-the-Japanese watched her differently. With a subtle and mysterious smile, the pupils of his narrow eyes laughing and piercing. As he reached the apex he would bend his knees vigorously, thrusting his companion still higher as she chased the rays of the setting sun.

How jealous we were! In six or seven years' time, we told ourselves, we would be like him, we would fly high above the courtyard so that a girl might be transformed into just such a parachute with fiery tresses. For the moment we were content to feel our hearts taking wing with the leaping heels, then tumbling back in blissful weightlessness.

Besides, we too had our share of heady joys more accessible to boys of our age. We would cross a piece of open ground, then another one, smaller and littered with old rusty scrap iron, and go down a steep path. Already on the way down we became aware of a strong scent of tar and the somewhat acrid reek of coal. The smells of the railway. We climbed onto a concrete barrier overgrown with giant nettles and waited.

The trains went by at full speed and we hardly ever managed to decipher their destinations. But sometimes, when a distant red eye lit up in the warm dusk, the train came to a halt. We studied the carriages eagerly. Behind the windows there was a life unfolding within the snug intimacy of the compartments that was totally foreign to our presence. One person was making his bed, another opening a bottle of mineral water. They drank tea, they read, they walked along the corridor with towels draped round their necks. All these people, who seemed not to have the faintest notion of the existence of our courtyard, fascinated us.

One day we saw a young officer at an open window with a pretty woman, whose acquaintance he had clearly just made. We could hear their voices in the quiet of the evening. The officer was talking in an offhand manner, very much at ease, making broad, sweeping gestures in the air. The woman looked at him with evident wonder.

'On the other hand,' he was saying, with raised eyebrows, 'when you've managed to pull your plane out of a dive, I can tell you, you feel a hell of a . . .'

The engine roared, the train lurched forward. The officer's last words were lost in the clatter of the wheels. We swallowed a regretful sigh.

'Leningrad to Sukhumi,' one of our number made out on an enamel plaque, then, when the last carriage had disappeared into the warm haze above the track he repeated dreamily: 'Sukhumi . . . That must be really something!'

We agreed with him, picturing this fabulous Sukhumi as a town of perpetual summer, inhabited by impressive officers and attractive young women who could be seduced with tales of dive bombing.

But the most remarkable event of that extraordinary summer took place at the very heart of our courtyard.

One day in early August a piercing cry obliterated all the other sounds, the peaceful, habitual sounds of an evening just like any other. This cry came from beside the Pit. The dominoes players broke off their game and turned their heads towards the thickets that surrounded the pool. The anxious faces of women appeared at windows. Old Zakharovna flapped her bony hand. We rushed towards the mythical location.

On arrival at the edge of the crater we remained rooted to the spot, faced with an inconceivable sight. The Pit had dried up.

Yes, it was empty, dry. And on its clay bottom stood a little boy, one of our gang, so dumbfounded he could not utter a word.

True, the heat that year had been quite exceptional. But this argument was not enough for us. It did not begin to match up to the significance of the Pit in the life of our buildings. Particularly since this location was soon to suffer a quite extraordinary fate. One that would change the very appearance of our courtyard.

As luck would have it, this event had been preceded in an obscurely symbolic way by an apparently banal occurrence.

Some days before the surprising discovery a huge jolting van appeared in the Gap. The children recognized it at once and proclaimed at the tops of their voices: 'The cinema! The cinema!'

Indeed it was the travelling cinema that came at dusk once or twice a month in summer to show its films. As it happens, they were always very ordinary films. Never features. Documentaries about Arctic exploration, about the areas of Leningrad with a revolutionary past, or even about the construction of the great canal in the Karakum desert . . . Nevertheless we watched them with genuine pleasure. There was not a single television set among the inhabitants of the three buildings. The cinema in the town was a long way off and generally packed. Here the show was free and you did not even have to get up from the dominoes table. The lorry stopped just across from the players. People brought out chairs and stools, the children sat on the ground, some people even watched sitting on their bicycles.

That evening the subject of the film was markedly different. When the black and white flickering on the screen settled down we saw the title appearing in exaggerated lettering, designed to inspire fear:

The Threat of Atomic War

'The threat of atomic war!' repeated one of the dominoes players, for the benefit of the oldest and the youngest, who could not read. 'The devil take it!'

Then we saw an enormous mushroom cloud with a white cap revolving on a stem. With slightly tremulous solemnity the commentator observed: 'On the sixth of August 1945, American imperialism inscribed a new crime against humanity in its bloody annals . . . Hiroshima . . . On the ninth of August . . . Nagasaki . . . Hundreds of thousands of civilians . . .'

'Dear God, how terrible!' sighed one of the *babushkas* sitting in the front row.

'Mum, why isn't the plane moving?' shrilled a little boy twisting the handlebars of his bicycle.

'Hush, hush!' came several voices.

A simplified map of the world appeared on the screen. As the commentator's explanations unfolded, it gradually became covered with black spots, like the pustules from a fearsome plague. These were the military bases of the United States. From these black spots swift little arrows were launched towards the readily recognizable contours of our country, the poison darts of future nuclear attacks.

'Those filthy American swine!' growled one of the men at the dominoes table. 'And to think I greeted them with open arms on the Elbe . . .'

Once again, to illustrate the message more clearly, ruined buildings appeared, as well as the whitish mushroom, majestic and arrogant. The camera panned over a sequence of injured and blind victims, bodies with horrible burns.

'And the worst of it is that filthy stuff gets at you everywhere,' murmured a spectator over by the jasmine.

'Look, Mum,' a little girl sitting on her mother's knee cried out suddenly, pointing her finger at the screen, 'that man looks like Lyoshka-The-Japanese.'

'Be quiet, you little silly!' the mother rebuked her and then added, in a hesitant voice, half addressing the company at large. 'The thing is, it's not like during the last war. Now, you don't know how to protect yourself . . .'

The spoken commentary seemed to anticipate this question. On the screen and still within the context of a series of simple diagrams, a number of circles appeared, surrounding a kind of large asterisk: the epicentre of the explosion. Maintaining a severely scientific detachment and even, it seemed, betraying a certain relish in the exposition, the voice provided explanations. Thus, in the first circle, Zone One, it said, you would be burned alive. In the second, you would be killed instantly by the blast. All things considered, these first two zones were of very little interest. For in them you would die 'normally', the radioactivity would not have time to take effect on you . . .

Things became interesting from the third zone onwards. There, and especially in the subsequent circles, everything had to be taken into consideration: the period of exposure to radiation, the wind speed, the nature of your clothes and even the cracks in your windowpanes.

A glimmer of hope for survival began to dawn. People stared at the figures that now filled the screen. Percentages of radioactivity, distances in kilometres, acceptable doses of radiation.

Finally came the most practical part of the film which everyone had been waiting for impatiently.

'In every district of our country,' the voice assured us, 'shelters have been erected in accordance with a strictly scientific design that guarantees infallible protection against nuclear radiation.'

Incredulous exclamations could be heard.

'So where's our shelter, then?' demanded the woman with her little daughter on her knee. 'Where are we going to go? In the hutches with our rabbits? Come off it! We haven't got a shelter . . .'

'It's in Leningrad, your shelter, underneath the Smolny,' jeered somebody, taking advantage of the darkness . . .

The commentator, as if he foresaw just such a reaction, showed himself to be very understanding: 'It may well be that, as a result of moving, you now live a long way from any specially constructed shelter. In this case you should know that you can build a totally effective shelter yourselves . . .'

Two men in shirt-sleeves appeared on the screen and, with the enthusiastic agility of stakhanovite workers, began digging in the earth at the edge of a wood. Hardly had this shot faded when the men could be seen already snugly tucked away in their burrow. Its ceiling was reinforced with stakes and the inside was woven with pine branches. One of the survivors of the atomic war seemed to be flashing a smile at the audience before he pulled shut a panel of neatly dovetailed planks over the opening.

The figures showed that a layer of soil twenty centimetres thick excludes thirty-five per cent of radiation; and a layer forty centimetres thick, seventy per cent; with a metre of earth above your head you can be sure that one hundred per cent of the radiation will be absorbed by it.

'And what if you don't have a spade to hand?' a voice asked with a sigh.

But the commentator had foreseen this eventuality too.

The two stakhanovite survivors appeared once more. Their only equipment now was quite ordinary knives. Bent double, like reapers, they began cutting thick armfuls of rushes. In the background a little winding river could be seen.

'It is important to know,' the voice-over instructed, 'that rushes constitute an excellent natural barrier to radiation. A metre and a half of these stems will keep out up to forty-five per cent of the radiation . . .'

By now the two men were installed in a hut whose thick roof looked like that of a dwelling for gnomes.

This time the disapproval was unanimous.

'He's got a nerve. For a start you've got to find your river with all those rushes.'

'Forty-five per cent! And what about the rest? Is he saving it up for pudding or what?'

'It would take you two days to build a thatched cottage like that.'

But the film was already coming to an end. By way of a conclusion a quotation appeared with a leafy surround:

> 'We have a country to defend, the men to defend it, the arms to defend it.'
>
> J. Stalin.

So the film dated from before the thaw . . .

The last sentence, however resolute, had failed to dispel the doubts inspired by the rush shelter. People got up slowly, picked up their stools and, as if reluctantly, lugged them back to the main entrances.

'You'd have done better to bring us a film about Karakum, like last time,' one of the women said to the operator, as he closed the doors of his lorry. 'At least there were camels in it. And jerboas. The kids enjoyed that . . . But with all your bombs just before bedtime they won't sleep now, that's for sure. And then those rushes: it was laughable.'

'I bring what they give me,' replied the operator. 'And when it comes to the bomb, there's only one thing to do if there's an atomic attack . . .'

'What's that?'

The spectators all put down their stools and turned towards him.

'Wrap yourself in a white sheet and crawl to the nearest cemetery.'

The people laughed uncertainly, not sure of having understood.

'And why a white sheet?' asked the woman who had missed the jerboas.

'So as to be buried in a shroud, as befits an honest man!'

The operator guffawed, slammed the door and climbed up into his cabin. Lurching across the uneven ground of the courtyard, the lorry headed for the Gap.

'Don't worry,' said my father, trying to set people's minds at rest. 'Now, thanks to Fidel, we'll be able to plant our rockets right under their Yankee noses.'

'And that's if their working class hasn't already tipped them overboard – the whole imperialist bordello,' said Yasha, smiling.

We listened to them avidly. The Isle of Freedom no longer looked like a defenceless little fish. Now we saw the spines of our rockets bristling along its back. We were sure that Florida would break its yellow fang on these spikes.

'But all the same,' you said to me very seriously, 'we ought to try out the rush shelter. Suppose we put two metres on. Who knows, it might keep out a hundred per cent of the radiation.'

This plan never came to fruition. For a few days later the Pit was discovered all dried out. The film about atomic war would now reveal its strange symbolic significance . . .

That morning we hardly touched breakfast. A single idea obsessed us: to be the first to explore the bottom of the Pit.

Seven or eight of us gathered to trample on its slippery, muddy bottom that made a noise beneath the soles of our sandals like cupping glasses being pulled off a patient's back.

The frenzy of a gold rush was as nothing beside the feverishness with which we plunged into the bowels of this place, finally accessible. We jabbed rusty spades into it, requisitioned from among the junk in the sheds. We lifted rocks by means of levers. Some of us even grunted like animals, scrabbling at the slimy, brown interior with our nails. It had guarded its secret for too long, the Pit. Now we wanted to rip it out by force and without delay.

The jostling at the bottom of the crater was fierce. Heads banged together; elbows, in their frenzied movements, rammed noses; mud spurted out of everything. But the importance of our first discoveries led us to put up with the discomfort of the excavations. A huge shell case, a piece of barbed wire wrapped in shreds of rotten cloth, a gas mask with the glass broken, a skull. Treasures beyond price. They seemed to be leading us on towards a unique, major discovery, towards some fabulous object that was already slowly awakening within the mass of warm clay.

The thing wasted little time before showing itself. First of all in the form of an obstacle that blocked all our efforts, then as a sort of metallic flank, convex, greenish, whose smooth surface we uncovered little by little. We thought we must be dealing with a thick drainpipe embedded in the clay. We were disappointed. Had we shifted all that earth for a bit of ironwork such as you could find in abundance all over the open ground?

Suddenly a boy who was digging at one end of the pipe emitted a whistle of surprise. This part of the tube was growing narrower and had strange fins on it. We looked at it more closely.

'But it's a bomb!' you cried. 'An unexploded bomb!' We stepped back a pace. The stupid bit of piping had suddenly transformed itself into a great menacing beast, with its blackened stabilizers sticking up out of the earth . . .

Without being alerted, the adults began to gather about the crater, as if they had had an intuition of our discovery. In the frozen gaze they focused on the monster emerging from the clay we discerned the ghost of ancient terrors, of griefs from long ago.

Three hours later the Pit was surrounded by a rope

to which scraps of red cloth were tied. At the four corners of this area they set up notices: 'Danger'. Sappers were stripping away the undergrowth around the Pit and performing their arcane rituals.

Minutes ticked away unusually slowly and silently. The children were made to go indoors, the Gap was blocked by a lorry. It was strange to look out of the window and see the dominoes table unoccupied, the swing motionless, the *babushkas'* benches empty. Adults passing one another in the flat spoke in hushed tones.

Finally, a rumour filtered through the closed windows and doors. The bomb was embedded between two blocks of concrete. It could neither be defused on the spot nor extracted to be transported elsewhere . . .

People hesitated to raise the third possibility. But Yasha, assuming an air of comic alarm, dared to remark: 'If they explode it here in the courtyard we all run the risk of being allocated new flats. Separate ones! It's an ill wind that blows nobody any good, wouldn't you say?'

In the courtyard we saw several army officers appear for whom one of the sappers was clearly acting as guide. They inspected the Pit, and looked at the windows in our three buildings, shaking their heads and exchanging heavily significant glances. Two soldiers unrolled a decameter measuring chain between the edge of the Pit and the closest of the walls.

The following morning there could no longer be any doubt about it. We were woken up by the continuous clatter of pneumatic drills. Our noses pressed to the window, we saw the Pit flattened by a slab of concrete. Around its edges the soldiers were erecting a kind of wooden dome constructed from thick pine planks fastened to a broad skeleton.

'It's to screen off shrapnel,' explained my father in a grave voice.

So the third possibility had won the day.

The main business was carried out on Saturday. The inhabitants of the three buildings came out into the courtyard in an orderly manner and proceeded towards the army lorries that awaited them in the Gap. It looked as if we were simulating a wartime evacuation. The women carried little bags – iron rations for the whole family. The men assisted the most decrepit of the *babushkas*. The children, whose parents had made them wear warm clothes, no one knew why, frowned solemnly, happy to look grown-up. Yes, it was a real evacuation.

When we were all packed into the lorries a voice called out several times at the main entrances to the buildings: 'Is everyone out? Is anyone still there? Hullo! Hullo! Anybody?'

There was no reply. The lorries moved off.

They took us a couple of miles away. We got down in the middle of a field of rape without taking our eyes off the indistinct pinkish smudge formed in the distance by our three buildings. The military also kept the pink smudge under observation, consulting their watches with a preoccupation that was more assumed than real.

As we camped there everyone was convinced that the explosion would take place at a precise time, army fashion, on the dot of ten or eleven. Such rigour seemed to us quite essential for the gravity of the occasion to be properly felt.

However, eleven o'clock came and went and the sun grew hot but the air above the pink smudge still remained serenely clear. It was then that someone had this flash of inspiration: the explosion would take place at noon precisely, for it was at noon that the radio broadcast the bulletin with the latest news. In it the mystery of our Pit would doubtless enjoy a place of honour. Everyone was of the same opinion. We were surprised at not having thought of it earlier. Of course, it would be at twelve noon sharp.

Yasha, who was beginning to grow bored, then decided to test the accuracy of this forecast. He went to the officer for information . . . Yasha had not brought the straw hat he always wore in sunlight. He had thought our expedition would be over quickly. On his head he had now put a handkerchief, knotted tightly at the corners, with a large burdock leaf slipped underneath it. It was my father who had advised him to do this.

'I used to do it at the front,' he explained.

'Yes, you're quite right,' Yasha had said with a smile. 'The leaf wilts and absorbs part of the heat . . .'

With his handkerchief on his head he looked to the officer less like an evacuated flat-dweller than a typical holiday-maker. The stalk of the burdock leaf was sticking out over one ear, not unlike a snail's semi-transparent horn. The officer scowled at him.

'Comrade Captain,' asked Yasha, pretending to confuse the little star on the officer's epaulettes with the other kind, the large one: 'If it's not a military secret, when's the explosion due?'

The officer turned away so as not to see the snail's horn and replied between clenched teeth. 'Keep calm, citizen. No pointless questions. The exact timing of the operation is not to be relayed to all and sundry.'

'Tell me, at least, if it's for midday or later,' insisted Yasha.

'For midday? You must be joking. You've seen how much they still have to . . .'

At that very moment a cloud of dust and smoke made its appearance above the pink smudge of the three buildings. A few seconds later the ground shook beneath our feet and we heard the echoing roar of the explosion.

'Hey! That was a bigger bang than we expected,' exclaimed the officer. For a few moments he had become a normal human being again.

'But take care not to relay that information to all

and sundry, Comrade Second Lieutenant,' said Yasha, with a wink.

It was only towards evening that they took us back home. A scene of devastation met our eyes. The ground was strewn with fragments of timber, branches, the trunks of uprooted trees. On the site of the Pit we saw a crater twice as wide as before: in it the roots of several young poplar trees were sticking up into the air. Even the tall trees had not been spared: foliage thinned out, as in autumn, crowns smashed, branches dangling.

And, as the height of irony, the great wooden dome, half in pieces, had landed on the dominoes table.

Fortunately the night was warm. We swept up the fragments of windowpanes and went to bed in rooms open onto the strange nocturnal landscape of our ravaged courtyard. That night we felt closer than ever to its tormented soul.

Next morning, Sunday, two pieces of news emerged to underline the transformation of our communal life. First of all we learned that Zakharovna had not left the building at all during the explosion. She had simply remained in her flat and, taking advantage of her neighbours' absence, had bottled her tomatoes.

'Otherwise, I should never have had the kitchen to myself,' she explained.

The explosion seemed to have restored her wits. She spoke in a measured fashion and recounted in detail the preparations the sappers had made. People were dumbfounded.

'What did I tell you? It's an ill wind that blows nobody any good,' joked Yasha.

My father interpreted it in his own fashion.

'She told me one day, when I was still living at her place, that she'd seen a bomb fall close to her *izba* during the war. She heard it coming and flung herself to the ground. But there was no explosion. That happens. Very rarely, but it happens. And then a few days later she got a notice from the front. Her son had been blown up by a mine. She must have mixed up the two events in her mind. Ever since then she's had a screw loose . . . Now it's all right: everything's been shaken back into place . . .'

Our second surprise was the discovery that the sides of the former Pit were strewn with human remains. So the skull dug up at the time of our excavations was not the only one . . .

The local soviet's refuse collection department was not due to arrive until the next day, Monday. We had a whole day to examine the war relics, ripped out of the Pit by the explosion.

We began our exploration with the fear and respect that death inspires. We peered silently at the empty eye sockets, we poked at the brownish bones with the end of a branch. It was the jaws equipped with teeth and the noses that especially fascinated us.

'After all, they may be heroes,' you said. 'They

were defending Leningrad. They were the ones who stopped Hitler . . .'

You broke off suddenly. Just at our feet we saw a helmet. It had none of the even, somewhat naïve roundness that characterized our soldiers' helmets. Instead, it was equipped with panels designed to cover the temples of the soldier wearing it. For us this angular shape was an infallible sign. In all the war films, in all the pictures in our history books it was this helmet with side panels that crowned the silhouette of the enemy, the German.

'Look, here's one more', someone shouted, aiming a kick at another helmet with the same menacing shape that sent it rolling. 'And over there!'

At that moment from amongst the broken branches I picked up a badge: a flat eagle made of metal. And you were already scouring an iron cross with sand. So they were the bones of Germans!

Hardly had we understood this when a veritable rage for vengeance seized us. The big branches and the planks from the fragmented wooden dome were the instruments of our fury. The bones cracked under our blows, the skulls bowled along like footballs and shattered into fragments. We raised them high on our sticks before smashing them against the concrete blocks. We ground under our heels those very missing noses that, only a moment earlier, had inspired us with respectful fear. We crushed the dark eye sockets. We hurled the brownish ribs across the courtyard like boomerangs polished by time. And each of us vied with his comrade to break them with a louder crunch, to demolish them with one blow, to proclaim his victorious disgust louder than the others. We were waging our little war. We were making up for lost time.

'Stop that, you monsters.'

In our orgy of destruction we did not immediately hear Yasha's voice. We were gathered under a tree. Shouting and egging him on, we were lifting up one of our number who had had a brilliant idea: to stick a skull on the end of a broken branch.

'Stop that, I tell you!'

We turned round. Our sticks in our hands, standing amid the whitish shards, we waited.

'What do you think you're doing, you idiots?' asked Yasha with a slight quaver in his voice.

'What do you think? They're Germans! Can't you see?' retorted the eldest of our band, Gyenka-The-Brick. 'So, we're smashing their faces in. Any objections?'

'Stop that,' Yasha said again, and we saw that his cheek was trembling.

'Why? They're Germans!' yelled Gyenka defiantly, sure of himself. 'They're Hitlerites! Nazis!'

There was a moment of silence. It was a confrontation. We, proud of our victory, our muscles tensed in the desire to continue this enthusiastic massacre. And this man, thin, pale, his eyes sunken in dark sockets.

'They are dead people,' he finally said, very softly.

He had uttered these few words with such sorrowful simplicity that we stayed mute, overcome. Nobody dared reply.

'Help me gather all this up,' he added. 'We'll start with that.'

And Yasha pointed at the impaled skull.

We followed him silently. We gathered up all the debris of bones, all the skulls, all the helmets. Little by little the bottom of the crater disappeared under this mixture of relics. Yasha brought two spades. We threw the planks from the wooden dome onto the bones, we buried them under the earth. We tamped the earth down with our sandals. The Pit was no more . . .

On Monday morning a lorry tipped out a load of silky white sand on this spot. They constructed a sandpit for the children. Only the trees and the windows in the buildings bore the traces of the unveiled mystery of the Pit.

But the sequence of exceptional events that had disrupted the life of our courtyard did not end with the disappearance of the Pit. For on the very day the sand was delivered heavy clouds with the bluish luminosity of lead began to appear from the direction of the sea. With them they brought icy showers and piercing squalls, the end of summer.

These showers caught us unprepared. The windowpanes had not yet been fitted and the cold interiors of our beehives were filled with the iodized scent of the sea. It seemed to us as if, in a freak high tide, the waves had swept in over several dozen miles and were now breaking close to our courtyard just beyond the mist over the open ground.

Curiously enough, this inclement weather which lasted for several days gave rise to an unexpected flowering in our life as a community. We set to work and helped one another, became so close that we simply formed one big family, a united, energetic tribe, motivated by a cheerful will to survive.

Our three dwellings were transformed into a cave where, during these few long days and evenings, there reigned a somewhat primitive relish for the communal life. The delight of a fire in a great cast-iron stove, around which we gathered. The pleasure of hearing the wind hurling itself against the thin squares of plywood that blocked the broken windows. The happiness, for us children, of feeling ourselves protected by the grown-ups, who all of a sudden brimmed with solicitude and tenderness, as if it were everybody's birthday.

In our communal cave the reassuring sound of hammering was to be heard. The men came into the flats, sawed up plywood and nailed it to the windows. The women mopped up the flooded floors, lit the fires. Bowed under the icy squalls, the bravest spirits crossed the courtyard, bringing in damp wood from the shacks, and unloading it beside the stoves.

And in the smoke-filled kitchens no one was surprised to see people from all three dwellings gathered together at the same table.

One of these days was particularly bitter. Several times the rain turned to hail. The wind veered slightly and now, blowing at an angle, was managing to make its way in under the plywood through the cracks. What is more, the bakery where everyone in the courtyard stocked up with bread had already been closed for two days. The area round it looked like a deep and turbulent bog. An expedition to the town had to be organized.

We saw Yasha leaving the flat with my father. On the landing Yasha turned back and winked at our mothers, and at all the people with grave faces who were crowded into the corridor.

'If we're not back by this evening,' he said, with a grin, 'alert the captain of the ice-breaker Sedov. You never know in this weather . . .'

Even in the courtyard we could not see them, with all the windows blocked. We could only hear the noise of the *invalidka* muffled by the drumming of hailstones against the woodwork. It was an odd noise, too, somewhat reminiscent of water lapping against a boat as it struggled through high seas.

Our mothers pretended not to be anxious. But from time to time we noticed them glancing furtively at the clock.

The men returned after the murky glimmerings of

daylight through the cracks at the windows had faded. First of all Yasha set down my father. Then he brought an enormous sack up to our flat.

'Thirty-six!' he said in a breathless voice. 'One per flat.'

You told me it was the most delicious bread we had ever eaten. It was a little damp and smelled of cold fog and mighty winds.

One of the *babushkas* who came to collect her loaf smiled at Yasha and murmured in emotional tones: 'This is all so good! All in it together. just like in the war . . .'

Many years later I recalled this touchingly silly remark. So perhaps the dream we pursued as we marched towards the horizon did actually come to fruition. During those few days of life in the cave. In that primitive comfort. With that damp bread distributed by Yasha, a tired smile on his lips . . .

That winter, in the stillness of short, dark days, the courtyard seemed to be recovering little by little, nursing its wounds. The broken branches on the poplar trees were swathed in hoar-frost, deep snow hid the great mounds of clay thrown up by the explosion. Traceries of ice grew on the newly installed windowpanes. The December blizzards created high ridges of snow along the hedge, with the same configuration as in previous years.

Like a patient in recovery, weakened and anaemic, the courtyard was learning to breathe again.

In May our fears for its health were finally allayed. Within the space of a single night the poplar trees, butchered, decapitated, split in two, became covered with the bluish tinge of the first leaves. Their boughs were still quite transparent, the dead branches with their brown leaves still swayed in the warm winds and the sun-drenched showers. But already the triangle of the courtyard was filling up with the same verdant clarity, the same heady brew that nurtured all the sounds of communal life every summer, and fused them together in harmony.

The restored dominoes table rang with the din of pieces being slammed down. The damp depths of the thickets were alive with our cries. Out of the kitchen windows spilled the smells of fried onions and the clatter of washing-up. On the benches near each main entrance there was a gentle flow of somewhat indolent backbiting from the *babushkas*, who were gradually recovering their form after the enforced abstinence of winter. The swing carolled its *joie de vivre* and the newborn spring. The children dug in the mountain of white sand, forgetful of the Pit that had been there before. Above the Gap the first hints of our evening fantasies took shape in the sky. My mother's face appeared at a second-floor window and her ringing call penetrated beyond the bluish transparency of the first foliage: 'Yasha!'

This summer promised to be yet more marvellous than the one before. I had grown a good deal since the autumn. Like a dandelion tucked away against a wall: in springtime the sun changes its angle a little and the pale stem shoots up into infinite space, responding to this unexpected caress. Our instructor noticed this and from now on the honour fell to me to carry the flag for our troop.

Nor were you left out of these benign upheavals. It was your voice that now assured you of a distinguished role. Our chief singer stood down, a victim, like the rest of us, of the vexatious mutations affecting his vocal chords. Of all the troop you alone – and with surprising rapidity – had acquired a fine manly voice. Our unstable windpipes were still belching forth rattling sounds, emitting shrill whines, swelling with dull growls. But you would strike up the song, with perfect pitch and no wavering, in a velvety baritone.

We had grown. The luminous line of the horizon that inspired our passionate marching seemed close at hand. We understood almost everything in the dominoes players' conversations. No longer were the names of Stalin and Zhukov simply sounds in the communal cacophony. We were proud to see people from the town coming into our courtyard wanting to view the site of the explosion with their own eyes. They looked at us with respectful curiosity. We told them the details, drawing on the accounts of the sole witness, Zakharovna, and discreetly elaborating them. We felt we were grown-up, endowed with a history, a past . . .

And for the first time in our lives we believed we could sense a significance that had previously escaped us in the musical moaning of the swing . . .

'You won't need your tents any more this summer,' the instructor told us at the start of the spring. 'They've built a pioneer camp specially for you. A veritable palace! You'll see, there's everything: a ceremonial hall, sports pitches, a rifle range, everything!'

We started counting the days. Each morning the fresh foliage had grown more dense. The traces of the explosion became less and less visible. You obtained a tiny tube of red varnish and stained the cylinder of your drum. For my part, I polished my bugle until it became impossible to look at it in sunlight. These exciting preparations seemed to bring the summer closer. Waiting had become unbearable to us.

It was amid the vibrant and joyous notes of spring life awakening in the courtyard that an unthinkable event occurred. Yasha died . . .

He did this as he did everything – without attracting attention, without fuss. A stealthy death and for that reason all the more incomprehensible. It was as if he were afraid of marring the joy of this new spring. No one had any time to talk about his illness. He seemed to make a lightning transition from one day to the next and suddenly there he was, where all the residents, stunned, devastated, mute, saw him, on the morning of the funeral. In a simple coffin draped in red Turkey twill, laid on stools beside the entrance to the building. We were waiting for the hearse to arrive . . .

Yasha lay there, dressed in his dark suit that was familiar to us all. It was the one from school, from our mathematics lessons. There was nothing rigid about his pale face. His eyebrows were slightly raised, as if in amused surprise. His fingers were not clenched, petrified for all time, but simply and delicately interlaced. And on his breast, just above his little jacket pocket, you could see a white mark. During his lessons, absorbed in his explanations, he would often put a piece of chalk in this pocket.

No one could believe he was dead. The hearse stopped in the Gap. The band dissolved into shrill, grating notes. The coffin borne by men wearing dark shirts made its way across the courtyard. Our mothers walked together surrounded by the other residents. It was mine who wept, shaking her head and crushing a fist against her lips, her sobs drowned by the horrible clashing of the cymbals. Yours had no more tears. She walked slowly, as if she were testing the ground with her feet at each step. Her big eyes, with dark shadows under them, stared, unseeing, at the slight swaying of the coffin.

Yasha's face was turned towards the foliage that

once more covered the broken branches, towards the luminous glow of the clouds. And from his window on the second floor my father gazed at this face bathed in the light of spring.

His reddened eyes could discern something that no one else saw. Something essential, something ineffable. Was this not why, when the men thrust the coffin into the hearse, his head gestured a sorrowful 'no'. . .?

During the days that followed the burial you became a very special being for us. People spoke to you in low tones, avoiding your eyes. When you walked past the main entrance the *babushkas* broke off from their chat and sighed deeply, gently shaking their heads. It no longer occurred to any of your playmates or marching companions to tease you by mimicking your father's face.

You had been marked by the shadow of death. You knew the difference between the light of the clouds and the chatter of the swifts before and after. From now on you had the key to a whole realm in the past life of that universe we called 'our courtyard'.

This quite singular attitude towards you would no doubt have lasted much longer had another death, much more expected and comprehensible than Yasha's, not occurred four weeks later. That of my father.

Everything made it predictable. His absence throughout those four weeks from the bench overgrown by jasmine and dahlias. The ambulances that had stopped beside our main entrance on two or three occasions. A lengthy line of shoes waiting to be repaired arranged all along the wall of our room. The silence in his little cubby-hole. The darkness of drawn curtains. The sleepless nights. His heavy breathing.

His death took no one by surprise. The *babushkas*, those chroniclers of our communal life, interpreted the event with just that note of fatalism, characteristic of folk tales, that was needed to offer us all deeply convincing consolation.

'What do you expect? They were like a single man, Yasha and he. Once one was gone, the other couldn't tarry long . . .'

To tell the truth it was not the day of my father's funeral that was the saddest. On the contrary, that day, without admitting it to themselves, the residents of our three dwellings experienced a sorrowful feeling of relief.

No, it was one evening in May, in the middle of those four weeks that came between the two deaths. My mother, dazed by sleepless nights, her head buzzing with weariness, leaned out of the kitchen window, no doubt preparing to call us in for supper. She saw the fresh foliage, heard the mixed tumult of cries and familiar sounds. The harmony of the evening flowed along, as it always used to in its slow self-assurance. My mother smiled absent-mindedly and, without thinking what she was doing, called: 'Yasha!'

The whole courtyard froze in silence. The dominoes players were immobilized, their hands holding the pieces poised above the table. The *babushkas* lowered their eyes. The women stood up from their washboards, pricking up their ears at this call. We stopped our running and chasing through the bushes. It seemed as if even the twittering of the birds fell silent. Only somewhere on one of the floors a record player stuck in a worn groove repeated absurdly: 'My sorrow was known, my love, only to you . . . My sorrow was known, my love . . .'

Above the Gap, marble columns, vertiginous vaults, castles in the air towered up in silence. Our senses may have been dull, communal cave dwellers that we were, but they still picked up the echoes from that call, as they resonated in the unfathomable cavalcade of clouds.

We were conscious, you and I, of having been brought close by these two deaths. An unspoken bond that went beyond all those ties of comradeship woven casually in our games together. More than a childhood friendship, this shared experience marked us out in the merry band of our marching companions.

This bond, that had no need of words or protestations, manifested itself one day in a dramatic fashion.

We finally saw for ourselves the new pioneers'

camp, whose praises our instructor had been singing ever since the month of March. He had not lied. The whole was extremely impressive. A majestic white-washed building with two wings, dazzlingly white. A vast asphalt parade-ground capable of accommodating at least ten troops like ours. In the middle stood a gigantic flagpole equipped with a pulley mechanism for hoisting the flag. A football pitch. A rifle range. Loudspeakers that deluged the whole area with deafening, heroic music. And finally the main drive lined with thorny bushes in the midst of which, at regular intervals, stood plaster statues on cubic pedestals. Shotputters with enormous monolithic backs, female swimmers with monumental hips and thighs . . .

At the end of the drive, in front of the main entrance to the building, there arose a statue of Lenin made of the same immaculate plaster of Paris. It was as if the sculptor had endowed it with the same muscular verve, as a logical climax to his series of sportspeople. His legs apart, his fists grasping his cap and the lapel of his overcoat, Lenin was portrayed in a boxer's pose.

On the morning of this particular day, we were lined up in our ranks on the parade-ground. Each troop occupied a square clearly defined by white painted lines. A good pace in front of these serried ranks stood the bugler and the drummer. In front of our troop – the two of us. The male and female instructors, visibly on edge, paced up and down their squares, examining the ranks meticulously. A scarf carelessly tied, a button forgotten – nothing escaped their practised eyes.

The waiting lasted too long. One hour, two hours, time dissolved in the soft heat of the asphalt, the blinding slab of the façade. The word 'Inspection', whispered by the instructors, filtered through to us as it hung in the overheated air. But even without these intercepted whispers everything was plain. A visit by important personages, senior Party officials, was to mark this hot summer's day.

They made us sing the same songs repeatedly to give us something to do as we waited. They checked the straightness of our ranks once more and for the umpteenth time the tinny clatter of a final sound check – 'testing, one, two, three' – erupted from a loudspeaker.

At last they appeared. We saw three black cars drawing up in front of the main entrance. Half a dozen men struggled free from the padded seats, not without difficulty, and shook their stiff legs. They looked as if they had lunched copiously only a short time earlier. Red faces, loosened ties, glazed looks. They came and sat on chairs facing our squares and the ceremony began.

First of all our troops took several turns round the parade-ground, pounding the asphalt with their sandals and bawling out triumphal songs. But the asphalt was too soft. Instead of crisp, dry stamping, our footfalls produced slapping sounds, as if on a mass of well-risen dough. With their triumphant choruses the songs made our parched throats raw.

As it turned out, the men sitting on their chairs showed little interest in our noisy perambulations. They mopped their brows with their handkerchiefs and blew out their cheeks, stifling a yawn or a belch. Their drowsy eyes only became animated when one of the female instructors passed close by with bronzed legs beneath a little white skirt.

After the marching and the songs which, in the symbolic language of the ceremony, were supposed to signify our irresistible progress towards the radiant horizon, came the most important moment. We were to honour the flag. One by one each young troop leader marched up to the chief instructor, flourished his right arm in a pioneer salute, and announced that his troop was prepared.

When the red flag rose up the white mast the whole parade-ground exploded with drum rolls and bugle calls.

At the moment when the rectangle of red cloth halted at the top of the flagpole a kind of electric shock passed through our two heads. All the drums and the bugles fell silent, with the same disciplined crispness. But we, without conferring, without exchanging the slightest glance, continued to go full pelt at our instruments. Better than that, we redoubled our efforts!

To begin with they thought it was simple stupidity. Our instructor hissed at us in a furious whisper: 'Stop it, you idiots!' And he flashed a broad smile in the direction of the occupants of the chairs, as if to say: 'They got carried away . . . The impulsiveness of youth . . .' The latter also smiled, with the indulgence people have for an excess of zeal.

But the bellowing of the bugle and the rattle of the drum resumed louder than ever. Then an incredible suspicion filtered through the ranks of the participants. Was this conscious disobedience, a coup being staged?

While remaining at attention beneath the flagpole the chief instructor made a number of constrained but energetic gestures with his hands, and directed a silent grimace at the instructor for our troop. The latter hurried to pass on the message, twisting his mouth at us in turn and twice sliced the air with the flat of his hand: 'Stop!' The men on the chairs exchanged uneasy smiles, like adults who are beginning to find the mischief of children tiresome.

We hardly felt we were present on that overheated parade-ground. The orgy of sound was too intense. Dazzled by the glittering, brassy cascade, deafened by the thunder that made every cell in our bodies vibrate, we were far away. Somewhere beyond the bounds of the forests and meadows that swayed in the hot air. Somewhere beyond the horizon.

Already the instructors, overcome with fury, were

thrusting us out of the squares. Already snatching at our instruments. But as we wriggled within the grasp of hands that were carrying us almost bodily, we let fly our last roars from the bugle, extracted the final syncopated beats from the drum.

'This is sheer hooliganism!' whined a nasal voice from the chairs.

The door slammed behind us. We found ourselves in a tiny lumber room where the housekeeper kept her brushes, her cleaning cloths and her buckets . . . A narrow dusty window looked out onto a little courtyard where, in anticipation of the visit of the Party bosses, they had stacked up everything that was old, broken and ugly in the immaculate universe of this pioneer camp. Dismantled iron bedsteads, a wardrobe with smashed-in doors, several ripped mattresses. This heap was crowned with a large portrait in a broken frame, that of Marshal Voroshilov, who had fallen from grace several months previously.

Once the door had closed we were left alone. We were silent.

Our thoughts turned to the essential question, which, after what had happened, had acquired the clarity of an inescapable interrogation. Why all the marching and singing? Why all that fervour we were supposed to keep up day and night? In the name of what? For the glory of whom?

We were far from being little idiots intoxicated by

the abstract and ideal beauty of some 'ism'. Everything we appreciated in this world was, on the contrary, very material, concrete, palpable. From our parents we had learned a serene indifference to the ideological torrent that daily flowed from the airwaves, newspapers and public platforms.

We were far from being dupes. Had we not been witnesses to a scene repeated each time a new guest came into your room? Yasha would point to a photo on the wall and, without lowering his voice, would remark: 'And that's my uncle, a journalist. Killed at a camp in Kolyma by Stalin and company.'

He used to speak like that before the thaw, without hesitation, paying no attention to your mother's warnings, as she murmured in an anxious tone: 'Yasha, you know very well . . .'

Thanks to my father, we had little by little discovered the hidden face of the Great Victory. The shade of the triumphant generalissimo did not feature in our heroic dreams.

No, we were not dupes at all.

And yet every summer we would line up in our ranks once more and set off towards the radiant horizon. There was no pretence, no hypocrisy in our ringing songs that celebrated the young Red cavalryman and the workers of the world . . .

For if during our imprisonment in the little lumber room someone had put this simple question to us: 'In the name of what does the bugle sound and the drum roll ring out each summer?' the answer would have been simple too. We should have replied quite artlessly: 'In the name of our courtyard.'

Yes, in the name of those three red brick buildings constructed in a hurry on a terrain still riddled with steel from the war. In the name of the triangle of sky above them, in the name of the benches overgrown with jasmine. The dominoes table. The Gap.

In the name of the man with a great, pale cranium, the man who had been dragged out of a mass of frozen corpses. Within that mass, as it was slowly blanketed with gentle snowflakes from a Christmas story, one heart was silently beating. The only heart still alive in all that mass. That man had had incredible luck to be in the middle. Protected by the others. By the deaths of the others.

The bugle and the drum celebrated that incredible luck.

They also rang out in the name of a soldier. This man had stood alone beneath a sky that was breaking apart, falling back to earth in flames and fragments of red hot steel. The soldier, firing his rifle with a telescopic sight, was operating among craters that opened up with the precision of a well-prepared artillery bombardment. Sector after sector. To the left, to the right. Closer, further off. The earth was stripped bare beneath his feet, the trees flew into the air in flurries of leaves, leaving the soldier alone on the bare earth. He saw the village where a few moments before he had been selecting his living targets. Now in the ruins of the little houses there was no one left to kill. The soldier dived into a crater. He knew that the second shell never lands in a crater already dug. That's the probability. He obeyed this lifesaving rule instinctively. But the blast from a new shell flung him out again.

What would become of them, these two men? If you believed in probability . . . The first would remain an anonymous unit among thousands of frozen blocks. The second would be a wretched legless cripple, a drunkard who would one day be found dead in his crate on wheels.

Each summer the bellowing of the bugle and the rattle of the drum celebrated the slip these two men had given to the laws of probability.

In the name of what?

In the name of the silence of our mothers. As children we had managed to learn nothing from mine about Siberia or from yours about the siege of Leningrad.

'I'll tell you about it another time, it's all so long ago, first I need to remember . . .' they would say, and they told us nothing.

They knew that in a child's mind a mother must remain free from suffering, from tears, from harm.

In whose name?

In the name of those women who, in the midst of poverty and the humiliation of being crammed together communally, managed to carve out for us our share of childhood, of dreams, of sunlight. Your mother, as she carefully peeled the big potatoes, would tell us, as if it were a legend: 'And the most surprising thing is that on his way to the duel Pushkin passed his wife. Yes, their coaches went right by one another. If only she had seen him the duel could have been avoided. Just picture it! But sadly, she was short-sighted, like me . . .'

And in our room, while she was waiting for the laundry to thaw, my mother would talk to us about Siberia: 'In the village the front doors of the *izbas* always had a little opening, like a tiny window, and every evening the villagers would put out a piece of bread and a pot of milk for the travelling people. They never went to bed without doing it . . .'

'And the siege? And the prisons?'

'I'll tell you about it another time, it's all so long ago, first I need to remember . . .'

No, our singing was not hypocritical for we were singing out our happiness at being alive. Happiness at being born contrary to all the probabilities calculated by men of common sense and in contempt of all the wars invented by the makers of History. Happiness at being born, living and knowing that there is nothing better in this world than the measured words of a woman with red hands seated in a room perfumed with the snowy chill of linen covered in hoar-frost.

In the name of what?

In the name of that call that used to ring out on summer evenings above our courtyard.

'Yasha!'

When Yasha and my father came in all you could make out in the dusk was the silhouette of a single man – tall and well built.

In the name of that call . . .

When it began to grow dark in our storehouse we extracted two nails that had made the narrow window fast, gathered up our instruments and slipped outside. The whole camp was already asleep. Only the windows in the director's office remained lit. From there came bursts of laughter, the muffled tinkling of tableware, women's voices. Clearly the administration was trying to eradicate the bad impression made on the Party bosses by arranging a banquet.

'They must be having an absolute feast over there!' you remarked, smacking your lips.

We had had nothing to eat since the morning.

'You know, the best way not to feel hungry is to try and think of something else,' you advised me. 'You'll see, it'll pass, like the pain when you get a knock . . .'

We climbed onto the pile of gutted mattresses and tried to think of something else.

By the light of some streetlamps hidden behind the trees we could clearly make out the empty parade-ground, its huge, useless flagstaff, and the pale ghosts of the plaster athletes. Despite his stocky boxer's body, Lenin among his flower-beds was looking rather lonely.

Without exchanging a word we took up our instruments and the distant music, the weary saxophonist's blues, poured out softly over the drowsing camp.

This time it had new accents. In the murmuring of the brass and the soft moaning of the drum we felt we could make out some fresh truths that had never before occurred to our young minds, filled as they were with rousing songs and heroic films.

We were stunned to discover that the blues from the other end of the world could take shape even in this hostile milieu, lonely, imprisoned and hungry as we were. Yes, it could unfold its nocturnal lassitude even on a heap of gutted mattresses. Confronted by the stony gaze of a famous military leader fallen from grace, whose portrait, in its broken frame, lay at our feet . . .

The weary saxophonist was swaying somewhere beyond the oceans: the world we lived in no longer seemed unique to us. With sneaking, sacrilegious dread we contemplated a daring thought: the saxophonist on the edge of a tropical night might never have any desire to exchange his own weariness for the paradise we were prepared to impose on the whole planet. The paradise of the radiant horizon, the rousing songs and our communal life. This notion verged on blasphemy. We hastened to return to the bewitching drowsiness of the rhythm.

Its soporific beat was interrupted in an unexpected way.

The presentable face of our storehouse, the other side from the little courtyard-cum-dumping ground, looked out over a lawn with freshly mown grass. At its centre was a fountain sculpted in the same spectral plaster of Paris as the athletes and Lenin. Like the majority of fountains, it only issued forth its jets of water at times of great rain or, in the case of our camp, on the occasion of grand inspections by the Party. This fountain was all the less interesting because the lawn was strictly out of bounds. The two wooden benches located beside the fountain were purely ornamental in character.

That day, on account of the visit of the three black cars, the fountain was in continuous operation. Even after nightfall it went on spilling out gurgling water into its basin.

It was over this monotonous trickling that we heard the sound of footfalls accompanied by voices that seemed to be approaching. Our reflex was immediate. To topple off the soft mountain of mattresses, and creep back to the little open window of our gaol. We were sure we had heard the instructor's voice. We needed to return as quickly as possible to being resigned prisoners, conscious of the gravity of our offence.

I was the first to slip back into the cluttered space of the lumber room. Poised to follow me, you stopped suddenly, sitting astride the windowsill, your forefinger to your lips. We pricked up our ears. The voices were not coming any closer, the sound of the footfalls had stopped. You swung out of the window, and summoned me with a motion of your head. We skirted the wall of the storehouse and found ourselves a few yards away from the ornamental benches.

Our eyes, accustomed to the darkness, straight away noticed that one of them was occupied. We had no difficulty in recognizing the white skirt and blonde hair of the instructor Ludmilla. Beside her, or rather right up against her, sat a man whom our sharp young eyes quickly identified. It was one of the visitors from the Party.

In point of fact, to say that he was seated would be quite incorrect. His head, his hands and even his legs were aquiver with hasty thrusting movements. The extreme rapidity of his actions gave us the impression that he had several pairs of arms and legs and at least two heads. Ludmilla, it seemed, had her work cut out to resist the assault of these multiple limbs that embraced her waist, slid over her knees, clasped her hips. But did she in truth want to resist them? To judge by the speed with which she unbuttoned her blouse and raised the hem of her skirt – not all that much. The voice of the Party millipede was as feverish as his actions: 'But "later" when? Later – ha ha!

''Later'' is now! You're gorgeous. Ooh, you are gorgeous! No, no! There's no ''later''! Let me . . . Listen, you and I are no longer pioneers. He who dares not drinks no champagne! Look, everyone's asleep. What director? I don't give a fig for the director. If he shows up I'll drown him in the fountain. Do you know who I am? No, look. Just let me . . . Well, why not here? You know, I really like you! Oh that's just bourgeois prejudice . . . Undo it yourself if I'm hurting you . . . No, there's nobody there . . . It's just cats having a fling . . . Ooh, you're gorgeous! Don't worry, I'll put my jacket . . . Damn! That bloody fountain's made it all wet . . . Oh I do like you . . .'

Ludmilla's responses were rather more restrained. She confined herself to mentioning, between two playful grins, on the one hand the severity of the director and on the other the omnipresence of the caretaker. Finally even these convenient formulas gave out . . .

It was at this precise moment that the explosion occurred. Once again there was not the slightest element of conferring between us. No conspiratorial winks. No whispers exchanged. An impulse as percussive as an electric charge fused us together.

The bugle roared, the drum thundered. We emerged from the shadows.

I blew as I had never blown in my life before. The bugle no longer called, it yelled, it vociferated, burst into sobs. In its cry could be heard the death rattle of our extinguished young dreams. The wailing of a betrayed lover. The last hurrah of the desperado of the radiant paradise. The tragic bawling of the kamikaze of the impossible horizon.

You had left your drumsticks behind on the pile of gutted mattresses. The drum was transformed into a tom-tom with solemn, funereal vibrations. The beat had a penetrating power, a rhythm that, once heard does not leave you. This was what rooted the occupants of the ornamental bench to the spot out there on the forbidden lawn. They sat bolt upright and remained transfixed, much like the plaster statues.

The situation toppled over into catastrophe as a result of the caretaker's strict professional conscience. He had been drinking and then fallen asleep, tormented by remorse and doom-laden forebodings. At the first bugle calls he bounded out of his narrow iron bed, overwhelmed by the noise, and pressed down the levers for all the electric switches.

The camp was flooded with harsh, blinding light. Had not our instructor promised us that you could play football at night there?

It was under this pitiless light that the guests at the banquet, attracted by the clamour of our instruments, appeared on the lawn. The women with traces of make-up trickling down their wan faces, the men with glazed eyes, and features that seemed blurred and washed-out. Their resemblance to the plaster statues was striking.

We quickly perceived that our millipede was at the pinnacle of the hierarchy of these pallid pleasure-seekers. Seeing him in this delicate situation they swiftly snapped to attention in almost Pavlovian fashion.

Ludmilla was writhing, trying to pull down her skirt that had ridden up to her armpits. But the skirt was too tight and the new arrivals, stared in fascination at her long, tanned legs as they quivered in a strange, febrile and involuntary striptease.

It was while this was happening that the young troop leaders began to arrive at the double. No doubt they thought it was a night alert, an exercise we had been promised ever since the start of our visit. They arrived, having thrown on their clothes, their shirts unbuttoned, their knotted scarves awry. As they reached the lawn, deafened and blinded, they came to a halt, some in front of the chief instructor, some in front of Ludmilla, raising their right arms and yelling at the tops of their voices to drown our uproar: 'Always prepared!'

But in place of the time-honoured saluting response, the instructors bellowed: 'Get lost!'

The troop leaders, thinking they were living through a nightmare, froze in their turn into the same greenish, phosphorescent plaster.

The millipede, not noticing the flagrant disarray of his trousers, kept adjusting his tie with practised agility. The magnitude of the disaster had palpably clouded his brain. For he stamped and shouted out:

'Turn off that fountain at once! At once! Is this what you call the political education of youth? Turn off the fountain! At once! Turn it off!'

What he was really objecting to was you and me. And the blinding light. When the men standing to attention had finally managed to decode the sense of his Delphic commands the light was put out and we were hauled off to our dormitory. There in our bedside lockers were our iron rations: two slices of bread and a mug filled with cold tea.

Next morning we walked together down a country lane that led to the station. We were being sent home. The punishment could have been much more severe but in view of the importance of the personages implicated, our educators had decided to hush up the affair and get us off their hands as quickly as possible.

We walked along, our sandals throwing up warm dust, and from time to time we turned back to look at the white silhouette of the great building that dominated the plain. We carried our meagre luggage in two identical string bags. Like cowards, they had confiscated the bugle and drum while we slept.

It was an odd experience for us to walk along, shuffling our feet, stopping wherever we felt like it. No ranks. No flag. No songs. The sky was grey, low. The swifts were skimming over the ground. The meadows that ran down to a river gave off the strong, humid smell that precedes rain. We felt as if we were seeing and sensing all this for the first time in our lives.

What surprised us as well was the horizon. It continued quivering in the same place, even though we had turned our backs on our camp and were advancing in the opposite direction to that of our daily marches. So all is not lost, we thought.

'But it's sad, all the same,' you suddenly said in a low voice, without looking at me. 'It's sad . . .'

I tried to comfort you.

'Pooh! Don't worry about it. We'll join the paratroop section. It's a lot more interesting than marching about all day.'

You said nothing. You had meant something different. A minute later you raised your head, looked me in the eye and repeated with edgy insistence: 'It's sad. Ludmilla with that bloke . . . It's horrible!'

I gave you a quizzical look. But you broke off, lowered your head and walked faster.

It is true that you and I had very different temperaments. And besides we were all of us a bit in love with the beautiful Ludmilla.

Close to the little station where we were due to catch the train to Sestrovsk we passed a troop of pioneers who had just arrived. Their feet pounded the earth conscientiously, the bugle deafened passers-by, the drum faultlessly repeated its dull refrain.

We stared at them, dumbstruck. Their eyes open wide, their mouths tensed. And to think that only the day before we had looked just like them in every particular! It seemed incredible to us.

'He's thumping on it like a pneumatic drill,' you observed, gazing disdainfully at the drummer.

'And that one looks as if he's spitting into it,' I added, referring to the bugler.

We, too, spat with disgust and moved off towards the ticket windows.

On one of the last days in August the inhabitants of our three buildings witnessed a scene that definitively marked the end of an era in the history of the courtyard – as well as our own.

One peaceful evening, much like the others, a quarrel erupted at the dominoes table. The pieces flew. The explosive force of the oaths rose rapidly.

We saw big fists, heavy as bludgeons, swinging back and forth. The first bloodied face. A man on the ground. Hate-filled hisses. The shrill cries of women. The tears of frightened children. The protracted stamping, clumsy and ponderous, of men out of breath.

Finally they stopped. Confronting one another, their faces screwed up with hatred, their shirts in tatters, their lips bleeding. Filled with mutual loathing.

It was the hatred of those who suddenly see in others, as if in a mirror, the blind alley of their own lives. The fine promises for the future they have swallowed with trusting naïveté. The Great Victories they have been robbed of. The grand dream in the name of which they have spent all their lives in a poky hole in an anthill.

And so this brawl was inevitable. They had forgotten the magic word 'Pit' that in the old days used to mobilize the whole courtyard. Pit! Then a man with weary but smiling eyes would get up from his bench. He would walk over to the table, carrying another man on his back. He would set him down and then call out into the mass of shoulders already jostling one another: 'Right, lads. There's just time for one more game before the sputnik!'

A definitive page had been turned. And as all the real grand farewells are spoken lightly, in the cheerful confidence of meeting again very soon, our own leavetaking a year later was confined to several playful punches, a few trivial remarks, a nonchalant handshake. We were just fourteen. I was entering the Suvorov military academy, that nursery for the army. You were off to Leningrad to a mathematics school.

As we shook hands we mentioned various vague plans for the next holidays. We have not seen one another since . . .

I saw my mother for the last time a few days before leaving for Central Asia, where I was to take up my first posting.

It is a dream well worn from having been nurtured in the heads of so many more or less sentimental young officers: to walk across the courtyard of the dwelling where you spent your childhood, carelessly greeting those residents who recognize you, as they marvel at the greatcoat on your swelling torso and the crunch of your well-polished boots. I, too, was in thrall to that old dream.

It was not a particularly propitious day for this dazzling scenario of a return under the parental roof. All morning a light autumn drizzle had been embroidering the air with its fine grey dots. I took a bunch of roses. I was afraid they were a bit too faded. 'Will they still smell of anything?' I wondered anxiously. When there was no one around me I sniffed them furtively. They smelled of autumn leaves moistened with the 'Baltic' eau de Cologne I used to sprinkle on myself after shaving.

At the entrance to the courtyard, in the Gap, I saw a trench like one where they are laying gas pipes. It was partly flooded and surrounded by clods of earth covered in heel marks. So as not to dirty the boots of my old dream, I hugged the red brick wall.

The courtyard, with its bare poplar trees, its dominoes table, its benches dark with rain, seemed to me abandoned, shrunken.

There was nobody in our flat. I rang at yours. Before greeting me, as if to spare me even a second of anxious anticipation, your mother hastily declared:

'It's nothing serious, nothing serious! She's in hospital but there's nothing seriously wrong with her.'

I put my flowers down on the shelf in your corridor. At the top of the staircase I turned to ask: 'And Arkady? Does he come by from time to time?'

'Oh now he's in Moscow he mainly telephones to say he can't come . . .'

The old hospital in Sestrovsk was filled with the comings and goings of pallid patients in their crumpled pyjamas. Visitors could be seen sitting on the edges of beds taking apples and pots of jam out of their bags. The young nurse escorting me stopped half-way along a corridor and said to me: 'There!'

The wards were packed. Several beds had been lined up along the walls of the corridor. Among them was my mother's. To avoid her bedside locker obstructing the traffic they had stood it behind the metal bars at the head of her bed. After she had kissed me she stretched out her hand through the bars and picked up off the locker a semi-circular comb that she used to put in her hair.

What I saw on this night table was like a snapshot of our life in the old days. A strange encounter with familiar objects now standing guard over this bed against the long corridor with its cold, bare walls. The comb, a little mirror in a nickel-plated frame. And on the top shelf an old cup with a gilded edge half worn away.

We spent a moment engaged in a semblance of a

conversation made up of the assurances one gives as a matter of course, while scrutinizing the other's features, searching for imperceptible unadmitted signs.

In the dining-room somebody sounded a summons with the aid of an aluminium plate and a spoon.

'Dinner-time! Dinner-time!' a tremulous voice called out.

'Should you be going?' I asked, getting up from the chair the nurse had brought me.

'No, no . . . There's plenty of time,' my mother replied. 'There are three sittings. The dining-room's too small. I can go with the last lot . . .'

I sat down again. The corridor was filled with the procession of faded pyjamas, and the shuffling of slippers. All the patients carried their own cups.

I failed to notice the moment in our routine conversation when a story began to emerge, slow and interrupted by the words of people walking past. By the time I became aware of this, it was already well under way. I listened to her tale. I was touched and embarrassed to realize that my mother had begun to repeat the episode she had recounted to us on those Sundays when she was ironing. The one about the Siberian *izba* and the frozen milk brought on a snow-covered sledge.

My mouth tensed in a strained smile. I listened to her, filled with compassion for this old head whose hair had the transparency of greyish glass. The tale was repeated with painful precision. That of a scratched record, of a needle stuck in a worn groove, I thought. The sound of the sleigh bells in the frozen air, the grating of the runners, the noise of the hoofs, the crystalline milk . . . I was already preparing to interrupt her gently, to nudge her on towards another reminiscence, just as one nudges the arm of a record player.

But suddenly, while sticking to the simplicity of our winter evenings of long ago, the story took a different turn. Then I understood that my mother was in the process of confiding to me what in our childhood she had always avoided telling us: 'I'll tell you about it later. It's all so long ago, first I need to remember . . .' Now the time to relate the whole story had come . . .

Once again amid the frozen silence of the Siberian village there arose the tinkling of distant bells. Once again Lyuba, as everyone in the courtyard called my mother, heard the creak of runners and the clatter of hoofs on the ice. She told her mother. Her mother hastened to put on her sheepskin coat, and wrapped up her daughter; they went out. A horse, all blanketed in hoar-frost, already stood before the *izba*. Everything was repeated as in those tales of our childhood. Old Glebych grasped the glittering disc of milk in his mittens. He held it out to Lyuba's mother with her embroidered linen cloth, murmuring to her a verbal rigmarole of no interest to the little girl, a grown-up's remark . . .

Suddenly the great glistening disc slipped out of the

woman's hands! It even seemed to Lyuba as if her mother had let her arms give way on purpose.

The disc crashed onto the hardened snow of the path with a sharp crunch, shattered. Overcome with joyful amazement, Lyuba flung herself down to gather up all the fragments. In her haste she confused crystals of milk with lumps of ice. It seemed so important to her to gather up all the fragments down to the very last . . . Her mother was already drawing her towards the *izba*, repeating mechanically: 'Drop it, drop it, Lyuba. There's no time. Drop it! Let's go in quickly . . .'

Lyuba's father had been arrested the night before. Glebych had learned this from a neighbour, a woman in the town. He had reached the village an hour ahead of the two emissaries of the NKVD. Enough time for Lyuba's mother to pack her bags.

. . . The shattering of the milky crystal on the pathway in a Siberian village threw up a cascade of fragments reflecting a sequence of days, years, life histories all too readily foreseeable. They had become almost classic. The arrest of the mother; the 'boarding institution for the children of traitors to the fatherland' – that was the official name for the place where Lyuba spent her childhood – war, typhus, famine . . .

My mother spoke of these things in a simple and neutral tone of voice, like someone who has to do it to set her mind at rest. An admission such as you make once in your life and never speak of again.

To tell the truth, I was a little vexed with her because of this story. Did I feel cheated of my role as the dashing army officer? Disappointed not to be able to act out that old dream of the clatter of well-polished boots? The corridor was busy with the coming and going of young nurses who gazed admiringly at the elegant lieutenant with his cap on his knees and his greatcoat displaying its smart creases on the back of the chair. This past, now resurrected by way of a childhood story, seemed to be encroaching on my own youth, my own future. All the things my mother was telling me were already broadly known to me, as elements in the life histories of other people. To include them in our own family's past struck me as an unnecessary infliction of grief.

I looked at her dull eyes, her lips confiding this useless past to me with a feeble smile. 'Why is she telling me all this? What good does it do me to know this now?' I thought, with irritation.

For I was no longer the inquisitive child I had been, ready to share the burdens of others thanks to having no past of my own to bear. I accepted such sharing less and less. For in my past now there were helicopters that had crashed on manoeuvres, from which we had to extricate burned and crushed human flesh. There were the bodies of men whose parachutes had not opened, bodies that were like sacks filled with a mixture of blood and bones. 'Shut your traps and fold 'em neatly!' the sergeant would yell, rebuking the young soldiers who were being trained on the ground to lay out their harnesses. 'Or there's someone else who's going to 'ave to look for 'is teeth in 'is boots!' He knew what he was talking about.

What was slowly building up in my own past was that thick layer of experience that protects us from the pain of others . . .

When I left my mother I mistook the exit, and had to retrace my steps and walk back down her corridor. I was a little embarrassed at reappearing beside her bed. I saw her stretching her thin arm through the bars and taking her cup from the locker. The metallic clatter could be heard again from the dining-room. The people for the third sitting were moving along the corridor. As I approached I was still seeing this gesture: an arm reaching through the bars, a hand stretched out to pick up a cup. And at that moment I thought I could guess why she had decided to tell me the story of her life.

She saw me. She understood at once why I had reappeared: she withdrew her arm from the bars and smiled at me. Then, when I bent forward she lightly grasped the sleeve of my greatcoat and, without saying a word, brushed my temple with her lips.

I hated that first book of mine, you know, the one about the war in Afghanistan . . .

When I wrote it I took as my starting point actual events, which had all the disconcerting implausibility of real life. Introduced into a fictitious, totally invented, plot they sounded false, these hard, raw little facts. Yet it was the plot that had found favour and it was thanks to it that the manuscript had been accepted. The chapter titles, with their blatant symbolism, had been particularly well received. When they start to echo in my ears I shake my head violently. 'The Tanks are Drunk with Blood', 'The Hills Gutted with Death', 'A Captivity Longer than a Lifetime . . .'

If I had to rewrite that book now I should not devote a line of it to the battles or to my escape . . .

I should describe a single afternoon in a little village that our company had retaken from the resistance fighters. The soldiers moved forward, treading warily, from one house to the next. At the slightest noise they would fire brief, nervous bursts. If the noise came from inside a house they would toss a hand grenade in at the window. At random.

When I first encountered this practice, soon after my arrival in Afghanistan, I came down on them like a ton of bricks: 'You bastards! There may be people in there!' Then one day I saw a soldier who had not tossed in his grenade. He had come staggering out of the house with lowered eyes, staring at what he was trying to hold in with his hands. It was his guts, his belly sliced open by the blade of an old sword . . . The penultimate year of the war was coming to an end. The decision to withdraw the troops had already been taken. Each man wanted to survive at all costs.

They advanced, firing bursts at shadows, threw grenades, then went in.

In one of the houses, amid furniture dismembered by the explosion and spattered with blood, I came upon a pile of rags that was gently stirring. Incredulous, I poked it with the toe of my boot. The bundle of rags turned round. It was a child clothed in a long brown garment. Its face was burnt, its arms covered in shreds of torn skin. With the dread one has confronting a wounded bird – what am I going to do with it? – I took it in my arms and went out. The sergeant who had heard the whimpering from the bundle nestling in my arms said to me: 'Leave it, lieutenant! We're not going to get buggered up by a kid. Besides, it's burnt: it won't live.'

I knew he was right. Along the wall of the house there was a shelf of packed earth.

'Put it down there,' said the sergeant. 'If the Afghans come along they'll take it.'

He said that so I could abandon the child without scruples.

'No, no . . . I'll bring it,' I said, looking at the swollen face from which shrill wails arose.

'We've got four men wounded,' grumbled the sergeant. 'If the Mujahedin come for us in the gorges we'll be up shit creek.'

On our return the commandant gave me a withering glare: 'Where the hell do you think you are – Treptow Park? Which war do you think you're in?

Where are we going to stow that? The hospital's bursting at the seams . . . There you are playing at heroes and now the medics will go spare trying to find skin for a graft . . .'

I knew it had been an act of folly to take it with me. Which is what I should want to talk about now if I had to rewrite that first book. No question. About the folly you commit when you rescue a child.

After the book came out the French journalists took an interest in me. Is Islam the binding element for the resistance groups? Will Gorbachev be able to transform a military defeat into a political victory? How serious are the ethnic tensions at the heart of the Soviet army? These questions, each time in a slightly different combination, recurred from one interview to the next. After the first one I knew what kind of reply was expected.

One day I tried to talk about the child. I said that, once I had seen its burned face, Islam and Gorbachev no longer had any importance . . . There I was, carrying the child. Because of its burns I did not know if it was a baby girl or a boy. A burned child. That's all. A burned child among men crushed with weariness and hatred. A child in the arms of someone who does not know why he has encumbered himself with this burdensome little body. And the most astonishing thing was that the little bundle in my arms seemed to sense my hesitation. Seemed to sense that I was committing a folly in bringing it along. And, when, during the following night, we were travelling through the rocky gorges, it kept quiet. Yes, it no longer wailed, as if it did not want to provoke the others' anger. From time to time I would anxiously put my ear to its chest . . .

After this verbal sally the interviews became less frequent. Then the war came to an end. And, as happens with any product, stories about Afghanistan passed their sell-by date. As did my presence in the media.

There was another time in Sestrovsk: it was you I was hoping to find there . . .

After nine months' service in Afghanistan I was on leave. Those nine months had turned out to be quite enough to make me unused to life away from the war. As I walked through Leningrad I was unconsciously avoiding areas without cover. When the sun shone I would seek to hide my shadow within that of a tree or a house. Each sound I heard was the double of one that spelled danger.

I spent this month on leave living with a woman friend in Leningrad. All those days were filled with a bizarre mixture of hasty love – as if we were trying to build up a reserve of it – brief, violent quarrels and preparations for a trip to the Baltic coast, a trip that we constantly postponed, sometimes because of a quarrel, sometimes because of some hindrance at her work. We would gather up our beach things, make plans and then not leave.

In the end we never made the trip.

Two days before the end of my leave I decided – heaven knows why – to go to Sestrovsk. Which is to say that in fact I knew very well why, but the reason was an absurd one. I had recalled the officer and the young woman at the open window of the Leningrad-Sukhumi train. A concrete fence overgrown with nettles, our observation post. The pilot with his talk about pulling out of a dive. The pretty stranger's smiling admiration.

I asked my friend if she had a timetable for the suburban trains.

'A suburban train? For Sestrovsk?' she exclaimed in amazement. 'But you can go on the metro, it's twenty minutes from the centre!'

I was flabbergasted. To be able to go to Sestrovsk on the metro? The thing seemed inconceivable to me, unheard of. Almost against nature.

Yes, Sestrovsk had become the terminus for an underground line. I emerged facing the town's old cinema and ten minutes later I was going in through what in days gone by we used to call the Gap.

Two huge blocks of flats twenty storeys high had been erected at this opening. They looked like two enormous liners, slowly steaming into the triangle of our courtyard one behind the other. The first of them towered up where the dominoes table and the

Pit had been, the other was lodged in the Gap.

In any case the triangle itself no longer existed. One of the red brick buildings had been razed to the ground. Another looked uninhabited. Only our own still had curtains and pots of flowers at the windows.

Life around these white liners was now organized on a different plan, the key points of which were the new school, the supermarket's wide plate-glass windows and a bus stop on a route that ran across what used to be open ground.

I looked up, located the windows of our communal flat, then that of our room – the fourth from the left.

Your mother opened the door to me, did not seem to be surprised to see me, kissed me on the cheek. Her hair was of a fragile silvery whiteness, with long strands that she adjusted with a slightly trembling hand.

I followed her into the depths of the corridor, cluttered, as ever, with shelves, coatstands, cardboard boxes.

'No, but life is for living,' she said to me as she made the tea. 'And really, it's paradise here now. Just think what it was like when it was all under construction. They were driving in piles from dawn till dusk, the cranes were grinding away, the bulldozers were turning everything upside down. It's peace at last. And they've promised to rehouse us before the end of the year. It must give you a funny feeling, doesn't it, seeing our courtyard now?'

I nodded, smiling. In your room, however, nothing had changed. The portrait of Yasha's uncle on the wall, the rows of books, the clock.

'Look what I've saved,' your mother said, bringing out a box stored under the bed.

She dragged it close to my chair and opened it. I could not believe my eyes. It was those iron feet, the lasts my father used in his shoemending.

'When your mother died I couldn't throw them away. I don't know why . . .'

We drank our tea. Outside the window the great liner's multitude of glass panes glittered with hot reflections of the summer evening. Your mother had difficulty in speaking.

'It's my asthma,' she said, pausing to catch her breath. 'After all, I am the last of the old guard,' she added with a smile.

I noticed some thick bundles of letters on a set of shelves. She intercepted my look, her face lit up: 'That's my administrative correspondence. I haven't told you yet . . . I finally got them to put that plaque on the wall of the building. Well, on one of the buildings. It's a splendid victory, isn't it? A bit late, it's true. No one cares a jot about our ancient history these days . . .'

So it was, thanks to my wandering glance, that your mother came to tell me about the siege. 'I've never talked to Arkady about this,' she confided in me. 'As a child he was too sensitive. The smallest things upset him. And now when he comes to see me, it's always a whirlwind, we never really have time to talk. Wait, I'll put the water on to boil again . . .'

Your mother's name was Fayna Moysseyevna. I shall call her Faya, as everyone in the courtyard called her.

The Siege Building
(Ancient History)

She would doubtless never have survived, had it not been for that encounter in the depths of winter in a dark, icy block of flats. Yes, that young woman, Svetlana, whom the people in the flats always referred to with sly hints, winking at one another. Faya's grandmother had a kinder name for her, 'the merry spinster' . . .

Her parents had gone to Kiev to attend a cousin's wedding. Faya and her grandmother had gone with them to the station. The train had pulled out, her father's and mother's faces were pressed against the window. Faya had waved her arm, holding up a doll with a patched leg . . . It was 21 June 1941. Ten hours before the start of the war . . . That was the only memory she had of her parents – two loving faces pressed against the windowpane. The editorial in

Pravda that her grandmother had spread out that evening as she sat in her armchair carried the headline: 'The Workers' Summer Holidays' . . .

Faya was old enough to know that people were dying from two causes in the beleaguered city: hunger and cold. Her grandmother used to spend the night in her armchair. Like that it was easier for her to stoke the small stove in the corner of the room.

One day she did not get up. Neither during the night – Faya had not heard the scraping of the little door to the stove – nor in the morning. Her grandmother did not answer, did not stir, stayed in her armchair, her eyes half shut. With trembling fingers Faya touched the old woman's face. It was cold, rigid . . .

Then she set about covering the body with everything that was warm in that icy flat. She wrapped the armchair in two fleecy blankets, and on top of them she spread the heavy fur coat that her grandmother used to put on when she went out to fetch their bread ration. She even removed her thick mittens that she kept on all through the winter and put them onto her grandmother's numb, heavy hands. Faya was convinced that all this warmth must suffuse the frozen body, fill it with life. She knew that she must also fight against the second cause of death – hunger. But on the shelves of the little cupboard where her grandmother stored their bread, there were only a few small crumbs left. Faya gathered them up carefully one by one.

Next morning her grandmother still did not wake. Although Faya had so much hoped she would, especially in the morning . . . With the same wild hope she opened the door of the little cupboard again, but there were no longer even any crumbs there now. She tried to light the stove, could not manage it and went back to bed. She felt a strange mist sweeping over her. It seemed to her as if she no longer felt cold . . .

Svetlana found her curled up on the floor, close to the front door of the flat. She, too, lived on the fifth floor of this block. There was no one else left there: all the other inhabitants were dead, disappeared, gone. Most of the doors were left open: the blacked-out windows turned even the rare sunny days into twilight.

Before the war Svetlana had not been what malicious tongues claimed she was. Simply a 'merry spinster', liking men who did not count every rouble and enjoying the atmosphere of restaurants heavy with the smell of tobacco and spicy dishes.

At the height of the siege the military men passing through Leningrad, whom she used to meet on a street corner and bring to her room, were a means of survival. Should she have worked herself to death fourteen hours a day at the factory for a pound of bread like the others? Or dug anti-tank trenches? Or, worse still, scrambled over ice-covered roofs to put out incendiary bombs?

On their departure the officers would leave tinned food, bread, army biscuits on her table. One could live . . .

In Svetlana's room Faya would stoke up the stove till it was red hot by throwing in pieces of wood. They came from the most diverse objects: among them you could recognize chair legs, plinths ripped off and chopped up with an axe and even the struts of a toboggan. It was in this very search for wood that Svetlana had entered their flat, believing it to be long since empty.

The pieces of timber crackled, giving out fine sizzling sounds and radiating a pleasant heat into her pinched face. Soon the whole room was bathed in this comfortable warmth that made one forget the dark city outside the blacked-out windows. Fascinated by the ruddy dance of the flames, Faya stared, wide-eyed, yielding to blissful drowsiness.

It was the footfalls on the staircase that aroused her. She would jump to her feet, grasp the handle of the big kettle and put it on the stove. For 'the guest', as Svetlana used to say. The key clattered in the lock with an exaggerated noise – the agreed signal. Faya would already be concealed on a divan in a room tucked away at the end of the flat.

'See how warm it is here, my friend,' Svetlana's bright voice reached all the way to the divan, muffled by the icy air in the rooms. 'I stoked it till it was red hot just before going out. Hold on, give me your coat. I'll put it by the fire. Like that you'll be warm when you leave . . .'

Faya knew well the sequence of words and sounds she would hear. She lay in wait for the very last in the series, the clatter of boots in the corridor, the final click of the lock. Then she could appear in the doorway. Svetlana would be opening a tin and would simmer the contents in a little saucepan. They would sit down to eat. A whiff of tobacco hung over the room along with the rather sickly sweet smell of cheap perfume. Svetlana ate in silence, staring at the flames through the half-open door of the stove.

On occasion Faya asked her if she could go and see her grandmother. 'No, no!' Svetlana would reply in categorical tones: she seemed angry. 'She must stay on her own. I've locked the door.'

At these moments Svetlana's voice had a really nasty ring to it. Faya held her peace. She was afraid lest the 'merry spinster' should lose her temper and drive her out onto the cold landing. Before the war they used to say such things about her . . .

One evening Svetlana came back without 'the guest'. Sitting on the divan in the dark in that tucked-away room, Faya heard the hasty chink of the keys, rapid footfalls, a brief, raw cough like the bark of a dog. She saw Svetlana. Alone.

'I've caught one of these colds!' she told the child, between coughing fits.

Trying to smile, she began to prepare supper with the food that was left to them.

Svetlana was wearing an elegant, pale jacket. Too elegant for the dead streets. Too thin for the cold that turned the deserted avenues into slabs of ice with sharp, cutting corners.

Faya did not know how many nights and days were filled with that convulsive barking that shook the darkness of the room, with feverish murmurings, with hunger. After the abundance of recent times, this hunger was appalling, quite different from the dull listlessness with which Faya used to await a slice of bread brought by her grandmother.

One day an emaciated shape arose from the bed, shaken with feverish coughing. It staggered towards the shelves where the gifts from the guests used to be stored, felt along the shelf. Nothing. She looked at the child wrapped up in her blanket and said, in too loud a voice, as if she could not hear herself speak: 'Listen, Faya, I must go down. I must find something. Otherwise we're both going to snuff it here . . .'

Faya was afraid. It was the first time anyone had spoken bluntly to her like that, as if to a grown-up. She heard Svetlana dressing in the corridor, cursing softly; her movements were clumsy, things would not do what they were supposed to do.

'Light the stove!' she shouted, and slammed the door.

That night Svetlana did not come home. Faya opened the flat door onto the darkness of the landing, keeping her eyes peeled, pricking up her ears. She made her way through the frozen silence of the great dead dwelling, and took hold of the handle of the door opposite, the door to their old flat. It was locked. Faya walked along as far as the staircase and whispered into the black void: 'Svetlana! Sveta . . .'

A protracted, lifelike echo rang out in the stairwell.

In the darkness she felt the treads with her feet and descended half a floor as far as the landing window. At this spot her fear diminished. Fragments of the broken pane, dangling from strips of paper, tinkled slightly in the wind. The beam of a searchlight raked the sky. Her hands clasped her rag doll. One day a hole had opened up in its pink heel and sawdust had trickled out. Faya was devastated. But while she was asleep her grandmother had neatly patched it up. The doll was particularly dear to her because of those few delicate stitches. Especially now . . .

Suddenly from the darkness of the lower floors she detected a grating noise. Faya pricked up her ears. But her primitive, animal sense of smell was ahead of her hearing and her whole being whispered to her: 'It's the scent of food!'

Yes! It was a smell of smoke, of a cooking fire. She leaned over the banister and made out a faint glow. Grasping the banister now, she began to go downstairs.

The glow filtered from a door on the second floor. Faya remained irresolute for a moment, then pushed it open timidly. Her head was troubled by the smell of food, which became almost unbearable in the passageway she now plunged into. The light was coming from another room right at the end. It was from there that the smoke wafted out, tickling her nostrils and tensing her jaws. Faya moved forward cautiously, stepping over piles of old newspapers, chairs without legs, a mound of broken plates. Finally she stopped in silence in front of the illuminated threshold.

The person who was in this room had noticed nothing. His back turned, his legs stretched out, he was sitting beside the stove. He opened it regularly to stoke it with firewood from the pile beside him. From time to time he scraped the glowing stove with a knife. It was this grating sound that Faya had heard from the landing. Then he began to eat. He chewed very noisily, choked. Faya stared at his padded jacket with its ragged back, his *shapka* pulled down over the back of his neck.

She was already preparing to ask softly: 'Little uncle, couldn't you give me just a tiny piece, too . . .?' when suddenly she noticed the presence of another man in the room. Lying close to the stove he looked as if he was asleep. But he was sleeping in a strange way, naked to the waist. Faya looked more closely at him and saw that one of his shoulders was missing. In place of it something grey projected out of a pinkish cavity.

She could no longer understand anything: the stove, the seated man with his back turned and the other man sleeping full length on the ground . . .

But everything became stranger still when the man with the padded jacket stretched out his arm and seemed to delve into the pink cavity and throw something onto the burning metal . . . Faya felt as if a spring, stretched to its full extent, had suddenly been released in her head. She felt she was about to understand something appalling, that could not be understood, that did not exist, should not exist!

The smoke seemed quite different from that of their stove at home. Heavy, acrid. She took a step backwards. But then the fragments of a china plate crunched beneath her felt boot. The man in the padded jacket turned round sharply . . .

It was a woman . . . Svetlana!

Fayna Moysseyevna came with me as far as the end of the courtyard. The windows of the great liners were ablaze now with liquid crimson reflections.

'That was the night my hands froze. It was the end of my piano lessons. I ran through the streets of Leningrad, yes, like a mad creature . . . My mittens were still on my grandmother's hands. I was picked up by the driver of an army lorry . . .'

We were moving slowly towards what in the old days had been the Gap. From time to time she stopped, to catch her breath. Beside our building there stood the last vestiges of the old shrubbery. A few clumps of jasmine. A hint of the tumbledown fence. All around the liner-blocks there seethed a life that I could not manage to associate with the red brick building we had just emerged from. Beside a row of garages there were men washing cars, plunging into the entrails of their engines. There were women pushing prams whose youthfulness astonished me. The balconies swirled with multi-coloured washing. Masses of children came hurtling off the little red plastic slide onto the sand.

Guessing my thoughts, your mother smiled at me.

'You know, Alyosha, I sometimes think they were right not to want to put that plaque on the siege building. You can't preserve that past for ever . . . I'm vexed with myself now. I shouldn't have told you all that ancient history . . .'

She fell silent. We took several steps without speaking.

'But you see,' she added, without looking at me . . . 'It's like in that Tibetan legend. The past is a dragon kept in a cage in the depths of a cave. You can't think about the dragon all the time. Otherwise you couldn't live your life . . . But from time to time you need to make sure the lock on the cage is in good repair. If it rusts away the dragon could break it and reappear more cruel and insatiable than ever. I really like that legend.'

We stopped in the Gap. The white liner engulfed us with its shadow and a mixture of sounds spilling out of the windows from the television sets.

'If Arkady comes to see me I'll give him your greetings,' your mother promised as she kissed me. Then suddenly she squeezed my elbow and whispered very swiftly, bringing her face close to mine: 'I know it's horrible now in Afghanistan. A massacre. Dirty and cowardly. But even in that filthy mess you must try to . . . You know what I mean . . .'

At the corner of the liner I looked back. With her head bowed, your mother was walking slowly along beside the remnants of the jasmine towards our entrance.

Two weeks later on a scorching summer afternoon, with my finger on the trigger, I stepped into a house where a grenade had just exploded. On the threshold of a room wrecked by the explosion I saw a bundle of rags gently stirring at my feet and emitting muffled wails . . .

I'm in the reception office at the publishing house. The switchboard operator has already signalled my arrival to the upper floors, where my fate will be determined. She juggles with two telephones, answers the calls that come flowing into her little glass cabin, taps away at her keyboard. Among the flood of visitors for the day can she identify those authors whose manuscripts are destined for refusal?

I have the strange, disturbing feeling of having committed a betrayal. The very weight of the manuscript that drags at the handle of my briefcase bears witness to this.

I have told all, described all, revealed all. I have kept nothing back. I have totally gutted the pathetic interiors of the three red brick dwellings. I have exposed their humble joys and futile sufferings to public view, like used goods displayed on a strip of pavement. I have delivered the lot.

And the irony is that, even so, I shall probably never receive my thirty pieces of silver!

You should despise me heartily now. Isn't that what true confessions are for?

Whereas you, I know, will never breathe a word to anyone about our past. You will bottle it all up. You will transform yourself into a mass of energy and forward planning and, as you set out to conquer your new world, there will be no holding you.

I know you will be successful. You will be successful with a disdainfully nonchalant air, as if to cock a snook at the success everyone craves. You will attain the sought after comfort, luxury even, that causes so many people's past lives simply to fade away.

Your sense of humour will be quite sufficient for you to fulfil the role to perfection, to excess, smiling as you continue to flirt with the kitsch of *the American way of life*. Your wife will be a ravishing blonde, with the glossy radiance of a fashion magazine. Your house – filled with thoroughbred objects, serious, steeped in their own importance, whose very functions will, on occasion, be unknown to you. What does it matter? Your wife will know. And when people see you slipping into the soft embrace of your car – first one arm, holding your jacket, then a leg, your head, your hand already reaching for the telephone – who will ever believe that this elegant man with greying hair and a relaxed smile was once the drummer for a pioneer troop mesmerized by the radiant horizon?

The ideal will have been achieved. The goal attained. The gamble paid off.

But there will be a fault line in this success . . .

For there will be a day when you are travelling along in the company of your wife and your friends somewhere on the coastline of the warm seas, perhaps even on that peninsula, that yellowish fang, which in the old days threatened the Isle of Freedom . . .

It is evening, the holiday atmosphere and a few drinks will make you a little mellow, a little pensive.

An unexpected question will touch on that past you have obstinately kept secret until now. This time you will speak. There will be smiles, amazement, teasing. Polite incomprehension, you will think. You will empty your glass, speak again, with the somewhat aggrieved insistence of a person who wants to be understood. Glances will be exchanged, eyebrows raised, several hands will hasten to top you up, with the solicitude reserved for the sick. You will speak faster, louder, explaining, justifying . . .

And you will be repeating my own confession! Then in the uneasy silence you will get up and walk away without another word, hearing your wife's voice behind your back: 'Pay no attention . . . it's an attack of nostalgia . . . You know what these Russians are like . . . with the life they had back there . . .'

At the wheel, driving your smart car headlong into the warm ocean breeze, you will explode into one of those horrible Russian oaths, whose resonance you had almost forgotten. It will embrace everything – your house with its thoroughbred objects, your wife's diets and cures and, above all, your car, which you will detest particularly when you think about that little garage your father once fixed up among our shacks.

And what will infuriate you the most is that this explosion will be quite pointless. For the gamble has paid off. The goal is attained. And the dreamed of ideal is that little relaxed and smiling world you have just turned your back on . . .

All the rest is simply the bluster of a one-time pioneer with a red scarf . . .

At the end of your drive you will sit down to eat in an obscure corner where the salty exhalations from the nocturnal ocean will keep you silent, discreet company. You will lose count of your drinks. Your breathless heart will stumble and skid, inundated with viscous liquid, but it will survive. Like one that kept on beating long ago within that mass of frozen bodies . . .

You'll see, one day we shall be quits. My commercialism . . . your bluster.

And besides . . . Besides, you should know that in this manuscript weighing heavy on my arm I have not told the most important thing. And I shall never tell it. It will remain between us like a pledge of reunion in the uncertain future of our buffeted lives. Like an echo of the electric charge that one day welded our two minds together, filled as they were with the dream of a radiant horizon . . .

. . . It was one morning long ago. One morning in that wonderful summer when the secret of that pond they used to call 'the Pit' (do you remember?) was revealed. The summer of our evacuation into the field of rape, the summer of the great rains and the damp bread . . . It was at the beginning of June in the first few days of our holidays. Before all those great events that were to shake the peaceful existence of our courtyard.

My mother woke me very early. The sky, which is never really dark during summer nights in the north, nevertheless had that ashen hue it takes on before sunrise. For a few moments I was puzzled. School? But why so early? And anyway, no, it was the holidays.

'Get dressed, your father and Yasha are waiting for you,' my mother said to me, smiling somewhat mysteriously. 'They're out in the courtyard already . . .'

'But what for?' I asked very sleepily.

'Run along and you'll see,' my mother replied with a look of mischief in her eye.

I gave my face a cat-lick in the kitchen, drank a bowl of warm milk and, with a hunk of bread in my hand, I tore downstairs.

The courtyard was still plunged in silence. There were blurred, nocturnal shadows deep at the heart of the shrubbery. The planks of the dominoes table had a black, wet, night-time gleam. The little clump of trees around the Pit gave off a muted rustling. The washing on the lines stretched out behind the jasmine had the misty pallor of ghosts.

In front of our sheds I saw the little *invalidka*, its windows misted up. For there were a lot of people inside! My father at the steering wheel, Yasha beside him and, between his knees – you, curled up, your hands clinging to the big handle beneath the windscreen. I felt outraged. I had been woken last of all, like a little child, the best seats were taken and no one had told me anything about the expedition. Furthermore, because of the steering wheel above my head, I should see nothing.

'So, where are you going?' I asked in a grumpy voice as I clambered onto the floor in front of my father's seat.

Apparently you knew nothing either, which cheered me up a little.

'You'll see,' my father said to me, exchanging sly glances with Yasha.

My bad mood was quickly dissipated. From the first backfirings of the overloaded little *invalidka*. As it left the courtyard the car filled the red brick enclosure with a deafening roar. And, thrown together by the lurching of its fragile steel chassis, we pictured the surprise of the residents. They must have woken with a start, opened their eyes wide and pointed their noses towards the dials of their alarm clocks. Then, realizing what was happening, they would have pulled the covers around them. And we imagined their delight at going back to sleep, confident that it had been a false alarm and they still had three good hours of rest ahead of them.

As it turned out, my perch had its advantages. It is true that I could not, like you, watch the road unwinding in front of us. I also had to duck my head when the steering wheel was turned. On the other hand, every time my father accelerated by pressing a curved lever, his rough palm rubbed against my ear. This gave me the feeling of participating fully in the driving of the car. Moreover, I also found time to rest my cheek against one of the knots in my father's trouser legs and watch through the crack between the door and the floor. First of all I saw the uniform grey strip of asphalt rushing past this crack, then an earth road. Finally, when we slowed down, and still through the same crack, long damp grasses and seed heads began to penetrate inside the car . . .

We stopped in the middle of an endless, silent plain, which at this early hour had the same ashen tonality as the sky. A few yards away we could see a solitary *izba*, fast asleep. Beyond it the dark shadow of a copse.

Subdued by this misty silence, we jumped, you and I, out of the smoke-filled warmth of the *invalidka*. Leaving our fathers in the vehicle, we began to charge across the tall grass of the meadows. It was steeped in cold dew and the stems that crunched beneath our feet seemed to burn our bare legs. The silence of the sleeping plain was so intense that our shouts froze close to our lips and gave rise to no resounding echoes. Only the dragonflies, woken by our running, striped the air with their frenzied flights.

We emerged onto the muddy bank of a river. Its dull, motionless surface reflected the dark stems of the reeds with an almost unreal precision. At our approach this smooth mirror became covered with little swift flashes – young pike were fleeing from under our sandals as we splashed along on the wet mud. Then we ran beside the water, stamping with our soles, preceded by little arrows that streaked across the sleeping mirror.

Finally, out of breath, and transfixed with an intoxicating chill, we retraced our path. We saw the *invalidka* parked close to the hedge and the little deserted courtyard of the *izba*. We pricked up our ears. It seemed as if we could hear our fathers' voices beyond the copse. We pictured them sitting on a tree-trunk, smoking and chatting peacefully. The idea of giving them a fright came to both of us at the same moment. Yes, to creep up slowly and stealthily, as we came round the copse and suddenly: 'Aha!' leap forward, waving our arms.

We moved forward, parting the tall stems with our hands, so that they would not snap under our feet. We skirted the copse. We sensed the presence of the two men close at hand. We broke into a run, hurtling towards them. But the shout never passed our lips . . .

Yasha was walking along with slow rhythmic steps, his head and shoulders thrown back. He was facing away from us. In his arms, folded across his belly, he was carrying my father. He had never carried him like that before. And my father, with broad and free strokes, was swinging a scythe. The grass trembled and fell in a broad silvery fan. They said nothing to one another. They seemed to have found their rhythm.

I turned to you and winked, as much as to say: 'Not bad, eh?' But suddenly I saw your lips trembling and your eyelids rapidly blinking. You turned away and began to run towards the river, shaking your head. I thought it was a game. I followed you. A few yards further on, like an aeroplane losing height, you dived into the grass, your face hidden in the crook of your arm. Sobs were bursting out between your clenched teeth. I nudged your elbow: 'Hey, what's the matter?'

You pushed my hand away with savage violence.

With a shrug I got up and retraced my footsteps. Apparently there was something you had grasped that escaped me . . .

Once more I saw our two fathers. I heard Yasha say in a merry tone: 'How are we doing, Pyotr? I don't suppose we've got as far as the Nevsky Prospekt, have we!'

I looked at his great, pale cranium. A thick dark vein throbbed on his temple. A deep weariness could be sensed in the curve of his back, his tensed legs.

They walked along, surrounded by the tart freshness of the cut grass. Flowers with their bright petals still asleep, muted, fell at their feet. They walked along and each swing of the dew-spangled blade carried them forward to meet the fragile, silent dawning of the day.

They walked along and seemed to be alone upon the earth. Far away, beyond the silvery undulations of the plain, a long mauve cloud was forming. The wind smelled of mud and the first chimney smoke. They were alone. All alone in the joyful and primitive boundlessness of that plain. All alone in the immensity of that northern sky . . .

One day, you know, we shall play it again, that soft melody from a night long ago. Do you remember our duet of brassy murmurings and the caress of drumming fingers? To learn it, we needed those cloud castles above the Gap, our courtyard and even the radiant horizon. But once learned, it could pour forth again wherever we might be. So long as there is a scrap of sky above our heads.